BE MY HUMAN

JULIE LYNN HAYES
M.A. CHURCH

Dreamspinner Press

Published by
DREAMSPINNER PRESS

5032 Capital Circle SW, Suite 2, PMB# 279, Tallahassee, FL 32305-7886 USA
http://www.dreamspinnerpress.com/

Be My Human
© 2014 Julie Lynn Hayes and M.A. Church.

Cover Art
© 2014 L.C. Chase.
www.lcchase.com
Cover content is for illustrative purposes only and any person depicted on the cover is a model.

ISBN: 978-1-63216-158-1
Digital ISBN: 978-1-63216-159-8
Library of Congress Control Number: 2014945940
First Edition October 2014

Printed in the United States of America
∞
This paper meets the requirements of
ANSI/NISO Z39.48-1992 (Permanence of Paper).

To all of you who find aliens with stripes and tails sexy, lol!

—*M.A. Church*

To Jimmy, who loves Taz nearly as much as I do, and to the coffee that Taz loves to drink.

—*Julie Lynn Hayes*

ACKNOWLEDGMENTS

SPECIAL THANKS to Alicia Nordwell and Tali Spencer for their never-ending patience when it comes to being my beta and for keeping me sane at times. You ladies rock.

—M.A.

ONE

REED HAD Taz pressed against the door of their apartment, kissing him for all he was worth, when his cell went off. He recognized the little jangle that blared out of his phone as his mom's ring tone. Talk about being cockblocked in a major way.

"Need to answer that," Reed panted into Taz's mouth.

"Okay." Taz rubbed his body against Reed's, clutching at him.

"Shit, babe." Reed grabbed Taz's hands. He barely managed to stop Taz from shredding one of his better silk shirts. Those claws of his boyfriend's were something else.

The phone stopped ringing. Reed shrugged. Some things were more important than a phone conversation, right? Just as he resumed his exploration of Taz, the same damn song rang out again.

"Fuck!" Reed squirmed as he dug his cell out of his pants. "Just hold that thought, babe. This won't take long."

"I need," Taz whimpered.

"God, Taz, I know. Five minutes, tops. Promise. Let's sit down. Maybe that'll help."

He decided this was going to be the fastest conversation in recorded history. Reed answered the phone with high hopes, but slumped into a chair as he heard his mother launch into the same old same old. Did he say five minutes? What was he thinking?

"Mom, you know I miss you and Dad too." Reed switched his cell phone from one ear to the other, pushing back strands of his dirty blond hair as he did. He stretched out one long leg before him, wincing.

"What's wrong?" Taz flopped at his feet, gazing up in consternation.

Reed sighed, trying to calm his emotions. He'd never known a day could last so fucking long. Okay, part of that was his fault. Around lunchtime, he'd gotten the bright idea of plugging Taz with a remote controlled butt plug. Just a little bit of foreplay that would get them both in the mood for a fun night. A quick trip to the bathroom and the deed was done.

Little did he know what he'd just unleashed.

To say Taz had been hyped up all day was like saying it was mildly cold in the Arctic Circle. Reed's normally exuberant boyfriend had been flying high ever since, which meant he'd had his hands full of excited alien.

Thank God Taz's stripes hadn't been noticeable. At least he hoped not. Peter hadn't said anything, but being the soul of discretion that he was, Reed wondered if he would.

"Leg cramp," Reed mouthed, trying to focus on his conversation with his mother, ready to recite his yearly explanation of why he could not come down to Florida for Easter. Or Christmas, or Thanksgiving… or any other holiday known to man. He'd been having this same talk with Jeanette Hatcher ever since he'd moved to New York, when his parents had headed to a retirement community located in central Florida. After five years, some things never changed.

Taz instantly removed Reed's shoes and socks, then massaged his way up Reed's leg, beginning with the calf. Reed forced himself to stifle the moan that tried to work its way out of his throat.

"What? Yes, I'm listening." He attempted to ignore Taz's ministrations, but that was easier said than done.

"It's not cheap to fly down there, Mom. Plus I work late on Saturday. And the shop's open on Sunday. Well, no, not Easter

Sunday. But still, I have to be back on Monday again. That's a long way for one dinner."

Taz curled himself about Reed's leg, his focus shifting from soothing Reed's tired muscles to focusing on one muscle in particular. He could see what his crafty little alien was thinking just by the gleam in his gorgeous emerald eyes. Lord, not a good time, Taz. But he couldn't very well go and say that, and he didn't exactly want to. Which left him the option of getting his mother off the phone. Quickly.

Well, as quickly as humanly possible.

"I promise I'll make time to come visit just as soon as I can." He switched the phone again as Taz's fingers drew dangerously close to hallowed ground. How could he even think about being touched… in that way… while he had his mother on the line? *Jesus Christ. His mother!* He closed his eyes and swallowed hard. "Mom, I know I work too hard, but that's what you have to do when you're trying to succeed. Do I what? Have a boyfriend?"

What was she, psychic? Or had he given some inadvertent sign that he was happily in love?

"Um… um… well… yeah…." He knew what this would lead to and sure enough, ten seconds later, he heard her yell, "Herb! He's got a boyfriend!" He could hear his dad's voice in the background, calm and unruffled.

"Tell him I said congratulations."

"Your father says—"

"I heard. Thanks." Just then, Taz pressed his face into Reed's crotch, and Reed's mind went blank. A soft, throaty purr drifted up to him. "Oh shit!"

"Reed Hatcher!"

Oh God, he knew that tone of voice. He'd heard it often enough throughout his teen years, and even at the age of thirty, it still made him shudder. Well, that, and what was going on in his lap.

"S-sorry, Mom." Reed's eyes rolled back in his head as Taz rubbed his cheek against the fast growing bulge that *had* been going down. Until now.

"I need to get off here...." Reed cringed at his choice of words. "My battery's nearly dead. Talk to you later and I love you. Good ni—" Reed hit the end button and disconnected the call.

"You done already?" came an amused, muffled voice.

"Imp." Reed undid the braid Taz always wore, and threaded his fingers through the soft strands. That hair of Taz's was just beautiful. Reed suddenly tightened his grip and pulled Taz's face out of his lap.

Sexy green eyes looked up at him, the question in them clear.

Reed spread his legs a bit more. "Unzip me."

A flash of desire and a quick smile. Taz bent over him and got to work. At the sound of his zipper coming down, Reed struggled to control his breathing. The fabric of his pants parted, and then Taz dipped his warm fingers inside. Reed had been hard on and off since lunch, and Taz had been practically bouncing off the walls with desire.

TAZ HAD never realized how good need could feel until today. He'd needed Reed all day, and it was hard to understand why they could not simply go into the backroom, lock the door, and do what they wanted to do—namely fuck each other silly. He yearned for Reed to be inside of him badly... and yet it felt so good just to think about it too.

But now they were alone, and *now* they could do as they damn well pleased, as Reed would say.

He gripped Reed firmly, soaking in the warmth of his hardening cock, feeling it grow within his grasp. He loved everything about Reed and their life together, and he could not imagine an existence without him.

Reed's scent drove him wild, especially at times like now. Thanks to Reed, Taz seemed to stay in a state of perpetual heat, hard at a moment's notice. Ready to be mounted.

"Rawr!" With a cry, Taz moved his hand and buried his face in the opening of Reed's pants, practically inhaling his cock, his ass wriggling, as if by sheer dint of will, he could cause Reed's pants to disappear. The tip of Reed's cock touched the back of his throat, and he sucked at him, humming softly around the hard flesh of his mate.

"Oh God, Taz, the things you can do with that mouth." Reed arched his back, his hands clawing the armrests as his ass literally left the cushion. "Jesus, Mary, and Joseph, if you don't stop that I'm gonna come!" He caught his breath and slammed back down in the chair, his hands fisted in Taz's hair. One more second of that hot, wet mouth and he *was* going to come. His balls were already tight against his body, and his groin ached. "I'd love to come in your mouth, baby, but I'd rather be inside of you." As good as it would feel to come in Taz's mouth, he was determined to be inside Taz when he released.

Taz whimpered softly as he was urged off Reed's dick. "Please...."

"Bedroom. Now."

Taz leapt to his feet and shifted his weight impatiently as Reed stood. Once Reed was on his feet, he grabbed Reed's hand and pulled his lover to the bedroom. He barely got Reed inside the room before he yanked Reed's shirt off and ran his hands over the heated skin. Leaning forward, he nipped one of the hard peaks that were Reed's nipples. A husky groan emanated from Reed. Taz dropped to his knees and pulled Reed's pants and underwear down. With nothing between him and skin, he rubbed his cheek against the fine hairs of Reed's legs.

Reed stepped out of his pants and kicked them off to the side. "Too many clothes, babe."

"Yes, yes." Taz quickly unsnapped his own pants while Reed pulled off Taz's shirt. Taz toed off his shoes, one leg kicking madly when his pants got hung up.

"My stars, I can feel it every time I move. The plug," Taz moaned. "It feels like sparks are flying through my body."

His words only served to turn Reed on all the more. "So lovely." Reed traced a golden stripe that covered Taz's skin, eliciting more whimpers.

"Reed, when can we get the swing you told me about?" He ran his tongue up the inside of Reed's thighs, over the lightly haired delicate skin.

REED THOUGHT he might lose it then and there. The thought of having Taz in a swing stirred his imagination and his libido. But that was in the future, certainly not now. "We can't. Not yet," he panted. "I don't think this ceiling... will hold.... Oh shit...." Before he'd even finished speaking, Taz had pushed him down into one of the two chairs in the room.

"Want to ride you," Taz moaned. He turned about and bent over, presenting Reed with his plugged ass. "Pull it out, please. It's time for *you* to be inside me, not that...."

It was time, Reed agreed, as he carefully removed the toy. He couldn't help but think of its expensive counterpart, the overindulgent model that had originally brought them together, and he had to smile. This particular version, while not nearly as costly or sparkly, was perfect for their purposes and had done its job well, keeping Taz simmering all day long. Of course, to be honest, that hadn't been hard for Reed to do. Not when an occasional press of the remote control set Taz off as if he'd been goosed.

"Lube, babe," he murmured. "We need the lube." He lightly slapped that magnificent backside, remembering just how wonderful his lover's dark place tasted. "Hurry," he added, not sure how long he could keep himself under control. Taz lunged across the bed, not bothering to walk around it. He yanked out the drawer to the side table, spilling the contents on the carpet. Not taking time to pick anything up, he grabbed the tube of lube, rolled over, and returned to Reed's side, holding it out.

God, but Taz was gorgeous—that was the last coherent thought Reed had as he teased Taz with the plug, sliding it between his legs and rubbing against his balls, before tossing it aside on the table next to him. He spread the slick, cool lube on his dick, hoping the sudden cold would dampen his need to come, and grasped Taz's hip with one hand. Oh, Taz would ride all right, but he'd do it this way—facing away from him. Reed wanted to see his dick sliding in and out of that quivering hole.

"Straddle me, Taz." Reed held his dick as Taz scooted back, his legs on either side of Reed's. The two of them in that single chair was a tight fit, but Reed was determined to make it work. Even if the bed was just a few feet away. "That's it, babe. Slide down on that dick."

Taz groaned as he was pierced. Reed worked his cock slowly up Taz's ass, spreading him open and stretching him even more. Sharp little cries tumbled from his mouth as he worked himself farther down Reed's dick.

"Oh Reed, I'm so full." Taz threw his head back and moaned loudly once he was seated. He leaned back against Reed's chest, hands grabbing at the chair arms for support.

"So hot, babe. God, you are so warm inside. Feels good." Reed held Taz still, afraid that any little movement might throw him over the edge. Once the threat of coming passed, he nudged one of Taz's legs. "Climb on up here."

"You… you want my legs up here? In the…?"

"Yeah. Right here. That way you can use your legs and bounce to your little heart's content."

"Oh… oh yes…." Taz slowly lifted one leg, then the other, until he had both carefully situated in the chair. "Do I put my knees under me now?"

"Fuck, that feels good." Reed bit down on the inside of his cheek as the need to come rushed back, dagger sharp. Taz was totally impaled on his dick now. He hadn't figured out yet just how helpless he was going to be. "No, no, don't. Keep your feet under you. Now lean back and steady yourself with your arms. Yeah, like that. Then use your calves to help lift you as you ride me."

Reed placed both hands under Taz, grasping his pale flesh. He lifted him up and then let him drop back down onto his dick. They both moaned. "Get it now?"

"Oh, oh, oh…." Taz pulled himself up and dropped back onto Reed's erection. "But I can't reach my cock."

Reed grinned as his hands left Taz's ass. He palmed Taz's dick, his other hand sneaking around to tweak a nipple. "Exactly."

Taz's muscles involuntarily tightened about Reed's cock, even as his fingers gripped the arms of the chair harder. He pushed down, impaling himself as much as he possibly could on Reed's hardness, grinding his ass into Reed's crotch at the same time. He felt as if he'd been lit up inside, every nerve ending firing, sending out electric messages of pleasure through his system. He loved trying new positions with Reed, finding new ways for their bodies to fit together. This particular position had obvious problems—it permitted no kissing, and that was something to regret, for Taz loved to feel Reed's lips against his own.

"God, you're killing me," Reed moaned, his eyes rolling to the back of his head at Taz's sensuous gyrations against his already overheated flesh. He immediately regretted his words as Taz began to twist toward him, alarm overcasting his features.

"Shall I get off? I don't want to hurt you, Reed...."

Reed felt Taz's weight shift as he began to move up and off, but he quickly tightened his grip on the other man's cock—the only thing sure to get his attention and keep it. He really had to remember how literally Taz took everything he said.

"No, no, no, don't move. Not really. I didn't mean.... Oh shit, baby... you feel so damn good, that's what I mean, you sexy little cat you." There was no mistaking Taz's feline qualities as his calico stripes were very much in evidence now, and Reed thought he felt his tail attempting to manifest itself, although in Taz's current position, that might not work out so well.

Taz's purrs grew louder, and he ceased his attempts to vacate the premises. "You're so sexy," he murmured, leaning his head back.

"Me?" Surprised, Reed hissed through his teeth. "Sweetheart, you're the sexy one. Swear to God, there needs to be a mirror in here so I can see...."

Taz, satisfied he wasn't killing Reed, rocked slowly back and forth, dragging a low, deep sound from Reed.

"Mmm, do that again." Reed dropped his head back, his hands roaming Taz's body as pleasure rushed through him. Nothing in his life had ever felt like this. Ever felt this good.

Taz continued to gyrate his ass back and forth in Reed's lap. "Like that?"

"Um… yeah." Reed swallowed a laugh as Taz's tail put in an appearance, tickling him under his chin. "I like anything you do."

Taz grinned, then went back to bouncing up and down. That seemed to draw more interesting sounds out of Reed. Just as his legs were tiring, Reed grasped his hips and slammed up into him. Taz's body tingled as his orgasm edged nearer.

"Close…." Reed mumbled as Taz rode him.

Taz tightened his ass and bounced as hard as he could, his dick slapping against his stomach. He whimpered quietly. Reed wrapped his hand around Taz's dick and stroked furiously. Taz bit his lip as his orgasm built. With a sharp cry, Taz threw his head back and came over Reed's hand.

Reed grunted harshly as Taz squeezed him, triggering his own orgasm. "Oh God…." A few haphazard thrusts and he filled Taz completely.

Panting, he rested in the chair, waiting for his head to stop spinning. Taz leaned back against him. He laid his hand on Taz's chest, the purrs of his lover still vibrating under his palm. Happiness filled him as he closed his eyes. Everyone should get to know such joy, such contentment. Amused at how sentimental he was becoming, he opened his eyes. He might be all mushy now, but he had a reason to feel that way. And the reason was currently purring like mad in his lap.

"Guess we need to go get cleaned up."

"Okay."

Neither moved a muscle, both content to remain where they were.

"You mean right now?" Taz shifted and curled up in Reed's lap as best he could, a feat not made easy by the confines of the chair.

Reed stroked all that beautiful hair and kissed the side of Taz's neck. "Yeah, unless you want to sit here all night."

"I could do that."

Reed laughed and gently slapped Taz's leg. "Up, kitten."

Taz giggled and bounced up, all limber legs and grins. Once Reed was sure he could stand, he followed Taz up and into the bathroom for a quick shower. Which quickly turned into Round Two, although that consisted of more touching and tickling than lovemaking. By the time they finally finished their ablutions and dried one another off, they were both more than ready for slumber, and quickly fell asleep, making two contented spoons in their bed.

TWO

THE NEXT morning Reed stood at the bathroom sink, tying the green silk tie Taz was so fond of. "You about ready to go?" Reed asked for the third time.

"You bet." Taz pressed the remote for the nineteen-inch flat screen TV on the wall and watched it go black. He smoothed a crease in his gray dress pants. Reed had bought them from his own store, along with the black dress shirt he wore.

Taz loved all the clothes Reed had bought him; the soft textures felt so good. He'd already finished his morning allotment of coffee and had been channel surfing while he waited for Reed. He smiled appreciatively as Reed walked into the kitchen, suit coat hung over his arm. The suit fit Reed perfectly—he couldn't wait for them to get back home so he could remove it.

Reed saw the look in Taz's eyes and grinned. He fixed himself a cup of coffee to go and snapped the lid on. "After you, babe."

They'd been living together for a month now, ever since the fateful day Taz had literally fallen on Reed at the Empire State Building. One of the first things Reed had done after the adorable alien had moved in with him was buy Taz a cell phone, then teach him how to use it. Even though Taz was from another planet, one that was much more advanced than Earth, he was unfamiliar with Earth's comparatively primitive technology. Reed swore after Taz had been kidnapped by the creature he'd dubbed the Evil Alien, he'd always have a way to call for help, thus the phone. That first week after they'd been reunited, Taz had talked Reed into letting him stay home alone while Reed worked at the boutique. Bad idea. Very bad idea. Taz had called Reed around lunchtime, nearly in tears.

When Reed arrived home, he'd been greeted with a nightmare of a mess. Even before he got to his apartment, he could hear the TV blasting in the living room. Which was bad enough, but Taz had somehow figured out how to turn the surround sound on. When Reed opened the door, the noise nearly blew him out of his shoes. It was like sitting in the front row at a movie theater. That, it turned out, was the easiest problem to rectify. Reed had shut the TV off, then looked around the apartment, stunned and slightly horrified.

He'd forgotten about Taz's natural curiosity. What a mistake that was, and the proof of his error in judgment was spread out all over the kitchen. Flour had been strewn across the floor, a few eggs lay broken on the counter, every covered container in the refrigerator had been taken out and opened... then tasted. Taz had found the blender, dumped some sort of liquid in and turned it on, without putting the top on the machine. There was unrecognizable goo all over the counters, the cabinets, the floors. Plus, Taz had found the sugar. From the looks of it, he'd eaten half the bag.

And that was just the kitchen.

The bathroom had been thoroughly explored as well, as evidenced by the streams of shredded toilet paper spread throughout the place, toothpaste smeared all over the counters in minty globules, and so on.

What was that old saying about curiosity killed the cat?

Taz cried as Reed stood there, stunned, taking in the wanton destruction. Taz hadn't meant to make such a mess; he was just bored and curious. Reed automatically excused him. Taz had tried to clean up the apartment, but that only made things worse. He didn't know what bottles of liquids were meant to be used for cleaning. Finally he'd broken down and called Reed.

Reed had closed his eyes, taken a deep breath, then pulled a gummy Taz into his arms and calmed him down with his words and with his lips, gingerly stroking his slimy back. Reed had every intention of making Taz help with the cleanup... but Taz had turned green as Reed lectured him, and grabbed his stomach—which was making some of the most god-awful sounds Reed had ever heard. He spent the next thirty minutes holding Taz's hair out of the way as he threw up everything he'd tasted earlier. Once he got Taz settled in bed, he spent several hours cleaning up. Then he spent another hour logged on his laptop researching cat behavior. Granted, Taz was a man, but he did share some characteristics with his feline buddies. Except rather than sleeping most of the day away, Taz tended toward hyperactivity.

That was the last time Reed left Taz alone at the apartment.

A SHORT time later, they arrived at A Touch of Class. Reed held the taxi door open for Taz, who somehow managed to make even getting out of a cab look sexy. Peter had already opened the shop. There were no customers yet, but the day was young. Reed liked such quiet moments. He could sit in his office, with his computer and his bank statements, and try to make heads or tails of them, otherwise known as balancing the bank. Sometimes that was easier said than done.

First things first. He checked the deposits on the statement with what he'd entered in the accounting program, making sure everything matched. He entered the credit card deposits manually, which entailed adding them up first. One mistake and he'd be off, and then would come the fun task of finding the error, no matter how small. Afterward, he needed to add in the checks written, as well as the debit and credit card withdrawals. It made his head ache.

Reed jerked his head up. "Taz, what are you doing?" He'd been so engrossed in the receipts that he hadn't noticed when Taz slipped beneath the desk, snaking up between his legs.

"Who, me?" Taz asked with pseudo innocence.

"Taz, I'm trying to do this, okay?"

"Do what?" Taz laid his head on Reed's thigh, his fingers moving not very subtly toward Reed's crotch.

"It's called accounting. I have to make sure the debits and credits all balance so I can figure out if I have money in the bank. That kind of thing." He couldn't bring himself to squirm out of Taz's reach, but he was trying his best not to encourage him. Perhaps if he talked numbers, Taz's libido would give it a rest.

Somehow he knew better.

"Why do you want to do that?"

"Um, well, it comes in handy so I know how much I have to spend. And to make sure I don't bounce a check."

"What is a check, and how do you bounce it?"

"It's just a piece of paper that says pay this person X amount of money. If there isn't enough money in my account, the check bounces. Not literally," he hastened to add, knowing what Taz was undoubtedly thinking. "It's a figure of speech."

"Reed?" Peter stuck his head into the office. "Mr. I-Can't-Make-a-Move-Without-You is here. He wants your opinion on something. Got a minute?"

"Yeah, sure." Reed pushed back his chair, careful to make sure Taz wasn't in imminent danger of falling when he did, leaned down, and kissed him. "Right back, babe, okay?"

"That is a funny name." Taz gave him a querulous look, and Reed choked back a laugh.

"I'll tell you when I get back." Another kiss and he was off. Although the client in question was a pain in Reed's ass, he spent good money. This interruption would give him a chance to calm down from the excited state Taz had a habit of putting him into.

By the time he got back, he found Taz sitting at his desk, his eyes glued to the screen.

"Sorry I took so long," he apologized. "But he bought a lot of stuff, so—Hey, what are you doing?" He tried not to snap, but he could see Taz had been messing with things, and he had nightmare visions of having his whole accounting system locked up, inaccessible. Worse yet, needing to be entirely reentered.

He pulled Taz's chair toward him so he could get closer and see just what damage his kitten had inflicted.

"Reed, what's wrong?"

"It's just that…. I mean, I know you wouldn't do anything, but you don't know…." Reed was trying to find a delicate way of saying he was afraid Taz had fucked something up, without coming out and saying it, but words refused to come. Plus he was too intent on looking at the screen to comment.

"This system you use is very old, but I've studied it. It took me a few minutes to remember just what to do, but…."

"Whoa, hold on there, buddy. You what?" Reed's heart leapt into his throat. This was even worse than he'd imagined.

"I finished doing what you were doing, and—"

Oh God, this was the apartment all over again. But worse. Reed wanted to tear his hair out in great big handfuls, already mentally doing damage control. When did he back up last? Maybe if he rolled the computer back to that date, he could make everything right again. With a shaking hand, he began to scroll down the screen, looking for signs of something wrong….

He stared in amazement as he looked over the statement. It was perfect. Everything looked right and good. His mouth dropped open.

"Look, Reed, just one more thing to do." Taz reached around him, pushing the chair closer, and hit the button that said *balance*. And then the program did.

"Holy shit," Reed breathed, casting an appreciative glance toward Taz. So he was more than just a pretty face. Who knew?

"It wasn't that hard to do." Taz didn't get what the big deal was. Reed acted like he'd worked some kind of miracle.

Still stunned, Reed looked at the computer again. Amazing. In that second, he made a decision. "Babe, you want a job?"

"Are you serious?" Taz seemed befuddled. "Really? What kind of job?"

Reed pulled Taz out of the chair and into his arms. "Oh yes, I'm very serious. You're really good with this type of stuff, and frankly, I hate it. I hate numbers. Math was never my strong suit and this"—Reed waved his hand at the computer—"this is something I dread doing."

"Oh, stuff like this is easy, Reed. If you're sure you want me to do this for you...."

Reed kissed Taz's lips. "I wouldn't offer if I wasn't serious. Besides, you'd be saving me the headache of dealing with this stuff. Something that I would be very grateful for." *And it'll keep you occupied and out of trouble. And close to me.*

"Okay, sure." Taz nipped Reed's lips. He'd caught the "very grateful" part of that sentence. "It's really nothing special, you know. This is nothing compared to what I used to do."

BUSINESS WAS decent, nothing special, but nothing bad either. Especially for a Friday night, when most men were thinking of how to get out of their old clothes, not into new ones. Reed was satisfied with the day's take as they prepared to close shop. He and Peter stood together behind the counter, taking a quick last minute inventory. Taz was in the men's room. Once he came out, they were going somewhere to get a drink. Or ten. Reed was in the mood to have some fun. He knew Taz was always in the mood, a characteristic that endeared his sweet kitten to him all the more.

He opened his mouth and started to make a comment to Peter, when something in the other man's demeanor stopped him cold. He was just standing there, looking toward the street, but his eyes seemed so... lost. Lonely, even.

On an impulse, Reed asked, "Want to go out with us and grab a drink?" The look Peter turned upon him—a blend of happy and grateful—confirmed he'd done the right thing.

"Yeah, sure. I'd like that."

Taz bounced up at that moment, and Reed marveled anew at his constant high energy level. If only he could bottle that and market it... wow....

"Hey babe, Peter's going with us. Right after we make the night deposit." He didn't think that would be a problem with his lover. Taz liked Peter, and seemed to enjoy his company whenever he spent time at the boutique. Which was all the time now.

Taz smiled at Peter as he curled around Reed, snaking his hand into Reed's back pockets. "You are going to be artists with us, yes?"

Peter looked between the two men, confusion in his eyes.

Reed thought for a minute, then began to laugh. "No, no, not like that. I told him we're going to paint the town red," he explained for Peter's benefit. Damn, he really had to watch the expressions he used around Taz. He took them so literally. And he'd yet to find that book of slang he'd been looking for. Although, in all fairness, he hadn't searched for it very hard either. Sort of difficult to spend much time on the Internet when he was too busy making love to Taz on a regular basis. Not that he was complaining, mind you.

Reed finished with the night deposit and flagged a cab. There was a little bar not too far away called Timeout, which he really enjoyed. The atmosphere was gay friendly, the food simple, and the drinks reasonable. There was a nice-sized dance floor too, with tables off to the side. Most weekends there was a band. But what he really liked about it was the fact it was classier than the usual bar. The tables were dark wood and looked expensive. Each table had a decorative lamp with a Tiffany reproduction shade. Near the back was the main bar, set before a large gilded mirror. The place didn't have a "meat market" feel to it. Oh sure, there were both men and women on the make, but there were just as many couples looking to have a good time. The best part was they could talk—the music wasn't so loud it would make one's ears bleed.

Which was just what he needed. Peter might be his employee, but he was also a friend. That look he saw earlier in Peter's eyes worried him. Something was wrong, and now that he thought about it, he couldn't remember seeing Peter's other half, Henry, in a while.

Once everyone had settled at the table and ordered something to eat—no way was he letting Taz drink without food in his stomach—he focused on Peter.

"So, Peter, how's things?"

"You know how it is." Peter shrugged. "Eat, sleep, and work."

"Is that all you do?" Taz asked. "What about fun? Don't you have time for fun?"

Reed squeezed Taz's hand. He'd planned to ease into asking Peter about his love life, but since Taz had opened the door.... "Haven't seen much of Henry these days. How's he doing?"

Peter looked between the two men and then down, not answering immediately. Reed watched while he drummed his fingers on the table, his lips pressed together tightly. Finally, he released a sigh and glanced upward again. "We're not together now, so I guess you won't be seeing any more of him than I will. At least I hope not."

A large wave of sympathy washed over Reed at the pain evident in his friend's voice. He'd never exactly warmed up to Henry, but he'd kept Peter happy so Reed tolerated his presence in the boutique. There was just something about him that troubled Reed, though he could never put a name to it. He wasn't sorry to see him go, but he wished Peter didn't have to suffer like this, even if he was better off without him.

"I'm sorry," he said. "Want to talk about it?"

"Not much to tell. He told me he could do better, said I was boring, and I have no idea how to have fun. And then he moved on."

Taz leapt to his feet, and before Reed knew what he was about, he enveloped Peter in a large bear hug. "That Henry must be an idiot!" he fairly growled. "Some males are just jerks. I'm sorry he hurt you." He held an arm out toward Reed imperatively. Reed snorted—he got that message loud and clear. He pushed his chair back and joined them in their group hug.

"Good Lord." Peter chuckled when he found himself with his arms full of Taz. "Thanks, guys. I needed that."

Reed met Peter's eyes. "I am sorry, Peter. I feel like this is partly my fault. I've worked you as hard as I worked myself."

Peter sipped his drink. "That's true, but if the shop didn't take off, then I'd have been out of a job. So it was worth it, Reed. And besides, I like my job. Plus, I make pretty good money too." Peter grinned at Reed. "My boss is fairly easy to work with, and he gives good bonuses. Anyway, there's more to it than just how many hours I worked. He was tired of me, simply put."

"Well, the bull about you being boring is just that—bull. I've seen you cut loose with the best of them."

"What did you cut loose?" Taz asked.

Peter raised an eyebrow at Reed. Reed shrugged. He'd told Peter at the beginning that Taz was a foreigner, and that his grasp of American slang was very shaky. That was somewhat close to the truth. "What Reed means is I like to party as much as the next person. And I do. I like to dance, have a few drinks… things like that. I like to have fun."

"Oh, okay. I like to have fun too." Taz bounced in his seat. "Are we going to cut loose tonight?"

Both Reed and Peter laughed. Reed caught Taz's fingers and nipped the knuckles. "A little, but not too much. We all have to work tomorrow." Reed saw a waitress coming their way. "And speaking of that, why don't you let me order you a drink? I have a good idea of something you'd like."

"Do they make Reed-flavored drinks? I think I'd like that," Taz replied ingenuously as Reed resumed his seat after the hug. Instead of taking his place beside him, though, Taz climbed onto his lap and made himself comfortable, looking into Reed's hazel eyes. "I could drink you all day and all night, Reed…."

Reed felt his cheeks suffuse with heat for many reasons. It didn't help that Peter was snickering on the other side of the table, no matter how much he tried to disguise it as coughing. Reed knew exactly what Taz meant, and just thinking about Taz taking his cock into his talented mouth and sucking on it was making him hard.

Jesus, Taz, in public? Although a side of him he didn't realize he possessed was yelling *Go for it!*

And to make matters worse, the way Taz was squirming against him…. He needed to find a way to harness that energy into something designed not to embarrass him in a way he'd not experienced since puberty first reared its gay little head. From the corner of his eye, he caught a glimpse of wriggling bodies, and it was with a sense of purpose—and great relief—that he pointed toward the dance floor. "Wanna dance?"

Two seconds later, he found himself being pulled into the center of the action.

Reed found that Taz moved on the dance floor as sensually as he did in bed. Both men and women followed him with their eyes. He swayed to the music, his body undulating with the beat, his eyes heavy-lidded. Taz's long braid wrapped around his body and Reed wanted nothing more than to sink his hand in all that hair and pull Taz to him.

The dance floor lights flashed as the music pounded, vibrating through Reed's body—a primitive beat that set his blood boiling. All around them bodies pressed closer, but Reed only had eyes for the guy in his arms. Good God, Taz was one sexy man… male… and all his. With desire already flowing through his body, he jerked Taz around so they were positioned with Reed's chest to Taz's back. Reed settled his hands on Taz's slim hips and pulled him closer, careful not to make contact with certain parts. He didn't want to risk those stripes making an appearance, but he meant to make a statement: *this sexy guy belongs to me.*

After another couple of dances, he led Taz back to the table. Both were breathing hard. Okay, Reed was breathing hard, Taz wasn't even winded. No doubt about it, he was going to have to get in shape. A couple of dances and he was done. That wasn't going to work if he had any hope of keeping up with Taz.

"How about a little help here," Reed mumbled to Peter.

"You sure you don't mind?" Peter asked under his breath as Taz looked at the dance floor, the want clear in his eyes.

"I trust you." Reed meant every word. There were few he did trust, and Peter was at the top of that list.

"Oh, the waitress came by. I asked her to come back when we were all here...." Peter grinned. "And here she comes. Order me a Bud and let's split an appetizer. I'll see if I can help burn off some of this energy for you. And thanks, Reed. I love to dance. It's been so damn long."

Taz's face lit up when Peter motioned to the dance floor. After a quick glance at Reed and getting the okay, Taz was off again. First thing Reed noticed was the respectable distance Taz maintained from Peter.

Reed placed their orders, then sat back to enjoy the show. His mind jumped from one single guy to another, turning over several possibilities of potential dates he could set Peter up on—then promptly discarded each one. None were right for his friend. Peter needed someone who was as driven as he was, but who also had a fun side. Someone who understood that there were times work had to come first. And while it was on his mind, he made a mental note to ease up on Peter's schedule too. The guy was definitely owed some time off. No reason he couldn't give it to him, and what with Taz becoming a part of the business, who knew where they might be able to take things? *The sky's the limit.*

At the thought, he had to smile. He'd never appreciated the type of film that featured visitors from other galaxies—Peter was the actual sci-fi geek—but he suddenly found himself more interested in them. He'd have to ask Peter for some recommendations.

Just as the food arrived, Peter and Taz returned. Reed smirked, glad to see he wasn't the only one breathing hard after dancing with his kitten. He turned slightly in his chair, hoping Taz would get the hint that maybe straddling him in a public place wasn't the thing to do, but no such luck, as he sat smack dab on top of Reed and embraced him tightly.

Aw, who was Reed kidding? He loved it, loved the lap full of sexy kitten. The rest of the world be damned. Besides, this was one place where they were almost guaranteed to receive general approbation for their love. So what if he had to talk around Taz for now? He could manage.

"Need to catch your breath?" he teased Peter, but before the other man had a chance to reply, his cell phone went off. Damn miserable timing. He shifted Taz to one side and wriggled the phone out of his pocket, eyeing the number. What could his mom want at this hour of the night? He held it up to his ear, hoping he could hear over the sounds around them.

"Hello, Mom? What?" He listened intently. "Slow down, I can't understand you. When? Oh my God, yeah, yeah. As soon as I can get a flight out. Yeah, promise. Is he okay? Surgery? I'll call you back when I have a flight. I'll leave a message just in case your phone is off. Love you too, Mom." Sliding the phone shut, he patted Taz's ass. "We gotta go."

Across the table, Peter waited, a frown on his face. "Reed?"

Taz looked between the two men. "What's wrong?" he asked, rising obediently.

"We have to go, babe. That was my mom. Dad had a heart attack. He's at the hospital, and he's going to need surgery. We have to get home and pack. I gotta book a flight to Florida right away."

THREE

"OH GOD," Peter whispered in shock as Reed paid the bill. "A heart attack? Did you know he was having problems, or did this just come out of left field? Jesus, Reed, is he okay?"

"I had no idea. He's awake, and he knows what happened. They've got him medicated, of course, and they're running tests." Reed left a large tip on the credit card slip for the waitress, too distracted to do the actual math. "The heart attack wasn't that bad. Well, you know what I mean. He survived it. But Mom's freaked out, to say the least."

"I bet she is. What are you going to do?" Peter ran his hand through his dark hair, messing it up, as the three men walked out into the cool March air. "Man, I'm really sorry."

Reed flagged a taxi.

"I'm going to have to fly home. Damn, Peter, I hate dumping all this on you, but I need you to run the shop while I'm gone. I'm sorry, man. I *had* planned on giving you some time off. Instead, looks like I'm going to be upping your hours."

Peter held his hand up and flagged a second taxi for himself. "Hey, it's not a problem. I know that store as well as you do, and you know I can handle it. You just go and do whatever. I'll hold down the fort here for a long as you need me to. When are you leaving?"

"Tomorrow morning, I hope. All depends on when I can get a flight out. But I'm shooting for tomorrow. If you have any problems while I'm gone, you call me. I mean it."

"I will, but things should be good." Peter hugged Reed before he got in the cab. "Let me know something as soon as you can. I'll open tomorrow just like usual. And before you say anything, if I need to I'll call in someone to help me, don't worry. I got this end under control, Reed."

"Thanks, man."

Once Peter left, Taz turned to Reed. "Are you okay? You seem so calm, but according to my translator, a heart attack can be deadly."

Reed glanced around them, concern edging his voice. "Careful what you say in public, okay, babe? Let's just get home and we'll talk then." Reed ran a distracted hand through his hair. "I'm okay. Maybe just a little bit in shock, but I'm okay."

Taz laid a hand on Reed's arm before he could enter the taxi. "I'm here when you need me."

Reed kissed Taz quickly. "I know that, and I will need you... later. I refuse to fall apart on the street in front of everyone and their brother. That can come once I have a flight booked and I'm packed." *And probably will....*

Taz bundled Reed into the taxi and climbed in after him. Reed held him close and gently stroked his back.

"Am I coming with you?" Taz searched Reed's eyes.

"Absolutely," Reed reassured him. "No way in hell am I going down there without you."

Taz released a pent-up breath and burrowed into Reed. "I wouldn't want you to be alone. I'd worry too much without you."

"Hush you. Don't even think about it, it's not happening." Reed slid his fingers along the length of Taz's braid, calming himself with the familiar action. "My parents have a guest room. We can stay there and help take care of Mom. She's got a lot to deal with. And my dad...." He'd never considered it before, the question of his parents' mortality, and now here it was slapping him in the face. Sure, everyone died at some point. But he wasn't ready for that moment in time to be now.

He pulled Taz as close as he could and just held on for dear life. Oh Lord, what a way for Taz to meet his family. *Looks like Mom's going to have me home after all....*

After a few minutes of absorbing Taz's warmth, Reed reluctantly drew back, just far enough to pull out his phone so he could check on the first flight out. He found a search engine, put in the relevant data, and found a flight for seven in the morning, nonstop to Orlando. He got lucky, considering everything was last minute, to find an airline that offered bereavement discounts. From Orlando, they'd rent a car and drive the rest of the way to Lake Hydethorne, where his parents lived. He booked the flight and reserved the rental. That was all they could do at the moment, other than pack and try to get what rest they could. They'd have to be up in a few short hours to make that flight on time, go through all the preflight rigmarole.

Jeez, what would Taz say when he told him he'd have to take off his shoes and empty his pockets? Never mind, he'd deal with that later. The only blessing he could think of at the moment was that he'd had the foresight to get Taz fixed up with a fake ID. Otherwise he couldn't even think about taking him on a plane, not with the way security was anymore. It really helped to know people.

Back at the apartment, Reed set his phone on the coffee table and finally collapsed onto the sofa, pulling Taz with him. They lay there together for a long time without speaking.

Finally Taz spoke. "Tell me about your family, Reed."

Reed pulled Taz closer, stroking the colorful mane draped across his chest as Taz curled against him. "Well, let's see. My parents' names are Jeanette and Herb, and they're both sixty-five years old. They have three kids, me and my sister and brother. I grew up—well, we all did—in a small town in Mississippi. That's a ways south of here," he added for Taz's benefit; he knew his lover's knowledge of Earth geography was still rather limited. Taz had never traveled beyond the limits of New York City. "I went to college at a major university in Mississippi. Got my teaching degree. Not long after that, I moved up here and Mom and Dad moved to a small retirement community in Florida. My sister and brother live there too. Well, not in the community, but in the same city."

"Did you like living in a small town?"

"Pretty much. I didn't much care for the narrow-minded attitudes I ran across down there because I'm gay, but hell, you can find that most anywhere."

Taz frowned. "I just don't understand this kind of mentality some humans have. Same-sex relations are very common where I come from. On Trygos, no one treats anyone any differently for whom they love."

"You have no idea how lucky your people are, then." Reed shook his head. "I don't want to get into that right now or we'll be here all night. I will say I was lucky. My parents didn't give a damn who my partner was as long as I was happy."

Taz was quiet for a moment, then he spoke softly, "Do you think they'll like me?"

"Oh yeah, babe. They're just gonna love you." Reed kissed the top of Taz's head. "You'll be the first guy I've ever brought home. That alone should cheer Mom up. Unfortunately, as thrilled as I am at having you meet my parents and my sister, it also means you get to see my brother, Jacob."

"Is that a bad thing?" Taz lifted his head, regarding Reed quizzically. Reed couldn't help but think he looked just like an inquisitive little kitten. His little kitten.

"Yeah, I'm afraid it is, but I don't see any way around it." He released an exasperated sigh. "The trouble with my brother is he's got this permanent stick up his ass, and he makes no bones about telling me my choices are all wrong."

"Your choices? What do you mean?"

"About moving here to New York, opening a shop... being gay...."

"Being gay is a choice?" Taz wrinkled his nose in perplexity.

"No," Reed replied firmly. "It's not. My brother doesn't understand. Not me, not anything about me. Thank God Mom and Dad and Renee aren't like him."

Taz fell quiet as he played with Reed's chest hair. Finally, he said, "How does one get a permanent stick up one's ass? Is that like the plug you put in my ass?"

Reed had to work hard not to bray like a donkey. Although the laughter tried to well out, he managed to refrain. "No, not really," he said, yawning widely instead. "I'll tell you more about it on the flight. Why don't we get to bed while we can?"

"Sure. I can't wait to see what your flying machines look like."

"No doubt they'll be primitive by your standards." Reed laughed as he gently pushed Taz up so he could follow suit. Gaining his feet, he took Taz's hand and directed him toward the bedroom. "Tell you what," he offered as they removed all their clothes and slid beneath the blankets. "Play your cards right and maybe I'll make you a member of the Mile High Club."

"Oh, are we going to play cards on your flying machine?"

Reed stilled any further questions with a kiss as they settled in for slumber.

THE NEXT morning Reed woke well before dawn and started packing for himself and Taz. Taz was still sprawled across the bed, the sheet wrapped around his hips. Reed could see the cleft in his luscious ass through the taut fabric, and the knowledge of what was so close at hand spread heat through his veins.

Tempting, very tempting. As much as he wanted to jump Taz's bones, there just simply wasn't time to indulge. They needed to be at the airport well in advance of departure in order to get through the tangled skein of security.

Resolving to be strong, Reed fixed some coffee and then went to wake Taz. He sat on the bed, running his hands up and down Taz's back; he felt the muscles twitch beneath his palms. "Come on, babe. Need to get up, shower, and eat. We have a long day in front of us."

Taz stretched, his body uncoiling sensually. His eyes fluttered open as he glanced up at Reed. "Good morning."

"Morning," Reed answered softly. "Ready for coffee and something to eat?"

"Coffee?" Taz perked up.

Smiling, Reed ran his hand through all that thick hair. Who needed catnip? All he had to do was dangle coffee in front of Taz, and he had his attention. "Yeah, babe, coffee. Just as soon as you shower. And you have to eat too." That was his form of the carrot and the stick, calculated to prevent an argument, plus ensure Taz didn't ingest caffeine on an empty stomach. The last thing he needed was to have Taz bounce all over the plane. These days, they put people off of flights for what they considered erratic behavior.

Taz threw the sheet off his naked body, kissed Reed, and hurried to the shower. Just before he shut the door, he poked his head through the crack. "You were staring at my ass, weren't you?"

Bemused, Reed ran a hand through his hair. "Yeah. Can't help it. You have a fine ass."

A grin lit up Taz's face and he wiggled his eyebrows. "We have time for… you know?"

"No, we don't." Reed huffed out a breath. "Dammit."

"Then stop ogling my ass."

Reed let out a shout of laughter as Taz winked and slammed the door shut. He left the bedroom before he was tempted to see if Taz remembered to lock the bathroom door. Twenty minutes later, Taz was dressed in jeans and a light sweater and sitting down at the table to eat.

"Okay." Reed sipped his coffee as Taz plowed through breakfast. "I know I don't have to say this, but to be on the safe side… you're human."

Taz looked up. "I know that, Reed."

"I know you do, but I just needed to say it out loud."

"I understand the dangers." Taz patted Reed's hand. "I really do. I'll try to be careful what I say around your family."

"I'm going to tell them something that's as close to the truth as possible, just leaving out the alien bit." Reed nodded at Taz's breakfast. "Finish up, babe. The taxi should be here in about fifteen minutes. So, I'm going to tell them we met by accident at the Empire State Building, we decided we liked each other, and then we dated for a while. We'll be honest and tell them you're living with me now, and that you work for me too. The less we lie, the better."

Taz nodded. "Much better."

Reed relaxed into Taz's touch. How hard could this be, right? Taz had promised to be on his best behavior. Undoubtedly, Taz would charm his mother with his playful manner and high spirits. Not to mention, she would be happy that Reed was happy. His dad too. And Renee would be beyond happy, even if she teased the hell out of him. He pushed all thoughts of Jacob aside. They could deal with him when they got there. Hopefully, he'd keep his distance, although Reed suspected it would not be quite that easy. But if they could manage to coexist without fighting—especially under the circumstances—so much the better.

THANKS TO Reed's foresight, they arrived at the airport with plenty of time to spare, checked their luggage, got their tickets, and headed for the departure gate. Reed was afraid he might have trouble with Taz regarding the security measures, so he carefully explained everything in the cab on the drive, and by the time they got into line, Taz was well versed on procedure, if a little puzzled by the things that were expected of them. First hurdle jumped. *Now for the rest of the course.*

They got the okay to proceed and headed up the ramp, onto the airplane. Reed showed their tickets to a smiling brunette, who pointed them to their seats. The first inkling he had that all was not well in paradise was when he heard Taz's sudden intake of breath. He was directly behind the flight attendant, and Reed's immediate thought was maybe she'd said something to upset his kitten, although he couldn't imagine what. He soon found out the problem when Taz turned toward him, dismay written all over his face.

"Where's the rest of it?"

"Um, the rest of what?"

"Your spaceship. This can't be all of it, right?"

Jesus, Mary, and Joseph. Of all the things he'd schooled him about, it hadn't occurred to Reed to discuss the airplane itself. He'd just taken it for granted that an airplane was an airplane was…. And there he realized his mistake. Taz hadn't arrived in an airplane… duh. To him, this must be a very primitive vehicle indeed. But did he have to be so noisy about it?

"Um, babe, lower your voice, please." He placed his hand against the small of Taz's back, trying to will him into silence. Or at least a bit of discretion. Yeah, right. By now they'd arrived at their seats. Luckily the flight wasn't full, and they'd been able to obtain the two seats closest to the window. No one else appeared to be sitting in their row, so maybe they'd get lucky there. "Want to sit by the window?" He tried to distract Taz, at least until the brunette left. It worked for about ten seconds, until Taz parked his cute ass in the seat. Then he turned to Reed, just as the flight attendant leaned over to ask if they needed help with buckling. Reed got a funny feeling in his stomach as he caught a glimpse of something in Taz's eyes. He didn't know whether it was nerves or misgivings or what, but he just knew Taz was about to say something to give the game away in his misguided innocence.

"Reed, how can we possibly—"

That was as far as he got before Reed crushed his mouth against Taz's, kissing him quiet. He didn't let go until he felt Taz's muscles relax, and his tongue sought Reed's. Reed allowed him a little bit of play before he pushed back. The attendant was watching them with a slight blush and a friendly smile. Reed felt his own cheeks go warm, but luckily he'd managed to silence Taz. For the moment.

"If there's anything else I can do for you, let me know!" she said brightly before moving on to the next row of seats behind them. *Disaster averted, thank God.*

Reed caught his breath, pushed his fears aside, and leaned in to Taz, dropping his voice. "Don't worry, baby, everything's fine. I promise you. I've done this lots of times. Lots. Here, let's get buckled in. We'll be leaving soon." He helped Taz with his belt then secured his own. He was grateful the attendant hadn't tried to assist, as his encounter with Taz had left him quite hard. He slid his arm about Taz's shoulders, and they leaned together, hands joined as they watched the mandatory preflight instructions on the drop-down screen.

TAZ REALLY thought this mode of transportation was archaic and primitive, but he didn't want to appear rude when apparently this was the best the Earthlings could do. That certainly wasn't Reed's fault. So he thrust his doubts into the background and concentrated on being with Reed and keeping him happy. The seat was not the most comfortable. He'd much rather have lain on Reed's lap, but no matter how he squirmed, he found that there was no room to do so.

"What's wrong, baby?" Reed asked.

"I was just trying to lie in your lap." Taz thrust out his lower lip slightly, pouting.

"I know, I know." Reed tried to soothe him. "These seats aren't really made for that, I'm afraid."

"Silly seats," Taz muttered, as Reed squeezed his fingers. He released a soft sigh, rubbing his face against Reed's chest as he nuzzled him. "Soon, please?"

"Soon, sweetheart, soon."

Taz lapsed into silence, gazing at those passengers that fell within his field of vision if he didn't turn his head. Most seemed to be men in business suits, with a few women, and some young people of both sexes. He saw one human, he wasn't sure what sort of a costume he or she wore. It seemed to be a long dress, mostly black, a bit of white, and a head covering in the same shades.

The woman who'd shown them where to sit was going down the aisle, talking to the passengers, he noticed. When she reached the human in black, he heard her say "sister," and then he understood. Turning his head toward Reed, he commented, "It's nice of that lady's sister to travel with her on this unsa—" He caught Reed's look and hastily amended his words. "—nice airplane."

"What?" Reed gave him a baffled look, then gazed in the direction Taz pointed, a smile breaking out on his face that he quickly suppressed. "Oh, I'll explain later."

Explain what? Taz shrugged and remained quiet for about ten seconds. "Is there a bathroom here?" he asked.

"Oh yes, sure. It's in the back of the plane." He glanced up and noticed the sign to stay in your seats was lit. "But we're about to take off and you can't get up right now. Can you wait for a few minutes?"

"Sure," Taz huffed as the lady stood in front of them and droned on and on about safety procedures and emergency exits. Taz wanted to laugh out loud. If humans were as concerned about safety as they said they were, they wouldn't be on these things to begin with.

Their transportation jerked, then started an excruciatingly slow process of rolling to wherever it needed to go. Taz heard someone say taxi, which was confusing as this vehicle bore no relation to the ones he and Reed used on a regular basis. He watched as people zipped back and forth along the ground in little cart-like machines. The lady at the front finally sat down once she was finished with her safety speech. Taz had no idea what she'd said, not that it mattered. If this thing fell from the air, they would all die anyhow, so what was the point?

The aircraft made a turn and, as they approached a long strip of pavement, Taz watched another of these primitive things shudder down the strip then rise up in the air. Taz did some shuddering himself. This was their only method of flight? How in all the worlds did humans manage to even get to their moon? Yet Reed had assured him that people had done just that. Taz was baffled. What if this thing they were seated in didn't get off the ground? Could it stay intact upon impact? Did he really want to know?

Yes, he did. He leaned closer to Reed, careful to pitch his voice low. "How sturdy is this thing? Could we survive an impact while on the ground?"

Reed frowned at the direction Taz's thoughts were going. "Babe—"

"I have a right to know."

"I know, you're right, babe. Look, an aircraft on the ground is like any other land vehicle. Think of it like a big bus, okay? We'll either come to a stop or we'll hit something."

Taz watched as the plane across from him slowly rose into the air. It looked to him like it could fall out of the sky at any second. "Goodness."

He clenched the seat armrests as their aircraft waited the acceptable amount of time before takeoff, then lurched down the same type of strip. The whole craft jerked and bounced as it picked up speed. What in the name of all the stars had he gotten himself into? They wouldn't make it off the ground at this rate!

Reed leaned over and rested his hand on Taz's clenched fist. "This is normal, babe. Everything is going good. I know it's scary, but you're safer sitting here than in a car, actually."

"I'm never getting in another cab, then," Taz gritted out as he turned wide eyes to Reed.

Reed grinned and winked. "I said car, not cab. Big difference."

"Oh stars," Taz mumbled and glanced out the small window. He felt them lift off from the ground. It was a feeling he remembered from his childhood, like being lifted up by his dad—the strange sensation in the pit of his stomach that made him giggle. He'd let his hands swing out for just a moment… airborne. Now all that noisy bumpy stuff stopped and it got quieter. Taz meowed quietly. Would he ever see his parents again? His brother?

REED LOOKED at Taz. That little sound broke his heart. Taz was pale, sweating slightly, and he looked to be close to crying. This just wouldn't do. Reed knew of only one thing that would distract his kitten from his dire thoughts. He leaned into him, whispered softly in his ear.

"Hey, know what? When we get back, I'm going to tie you to the bed, babe. Then, while you're wiggling around on the mattress, I'm going to cut your clothes off. That's right, cut every piece of clothing off you... bit by bit. After I have you naked, I'm going to suck you until you're just about ready to come."

Taz's head jerked around.

"Then I'm going to plug you good, baby. Know that plug you like that vibrates so fast? I'm going to bury that up your ass and make sure it's against your hot spot. Then...." Reed blew in Taz's ear. "Then, I'm going to ride you. Yeah, I'm going to sink down on that dick of yours until you're balls deep in me. I'm going to ride you until we both come."

TAZ STARED at his lover in shock, everything forgotten but the picture Reed had painted. Taz bit his lip. Reed hardly ever bottomed, and the thought had his head spinning. "Oh gods, Reed!"

They were still staring at each other when, moments later, Taz heard a "thunk."

"What was that?"

"Landing gear going up into the plane. That's normal, no worries."

Taz looked out the small window again. There were clouds outside his window. "This is insane, you have to know that. Dangerous, insane, and can we please find a cab and go back home?"

"You're okay, Taz. Look out the window now. We're above the clouds."

"Very nice," Taz muttered. "And still insane." He didn't bother to mention the other problem he had now thanks to Reed's description of their future activities.

"The overhead light's off, so we can move around now. C'mon, I'll show you where the bathroom is." Reed helped him unbuckle himself from the constraint, and they stood. Taz followed

Reed to the back end of the small flying machine where he saw four doors, two on either side of the aisle.

"Right through there." Reed gestured to one of the doors. A skeptical Taz opened the door and glanced inside.

"This?"

"That, yes. It's small, I know, but big enough for—"

His words were cut off when Taz quickly stepped inside the tiny room, pulled Reed in, and closed the door after them.

Wow. Small was certainly an understatement. This room was tiny.

"Taz, what the hell?" Reed reached for the door, but Taz whimpered. He pressed one hand against Reed's crotch, feeling him harden beneath his palm. "No, Taz, not here...." he protested, but the words sounded hollow, even to himself. "Jeez, Taz... Can you just pee and we can go?"

Too late. Taz's stripes were beginning to show—orange and brown and gold. How the hell could they walk back out there like this? And Jesus, he'd caused this himself too, trying to distract Taz earlier. As if he could read his mind, Taz turned himself around—how, Reed wasn't sure, within that very narrow, confined space—and Reed heard the sound of a zipper, followed by the rustle of Taz's pants as they dropped to the floor, revealing his very delicious, bare ass. Reed's own erection began to bulge, straining to be free. He shook his head. At this point, he saw two choices, and one wasn't really an option—namely, backing out of the toilet and taking his seat and hoping Taz followed.

Then there was door number two....

His hands seemed possessed of a mind of their own as they reached for Taz's lovely striped ass. It was right there, so close at hand, so delectable, and common sense said that if they didn't deal with their mutually horny conditions right now, and quickly, they'd simply suffer for the rest of the trip. Handling Taz's fears about flying was bad enough without adding hot and horny to the list.

It wasn't like he didn't want Taz. Of course he did. He just hadn't thought he'd really be inaugurating him into the damn Mile High Club while on an emergency trip to see his parents, despite joking about the possibility. He stroked Taz's cheeks, watched the color in his flesh deepen. It felt good to know he was responsible for that, to know that Taz wanted him every bit as much as he wanted Taz.

"All right," he capitulated, "all right. But we can't afford finesse right now. It's gotta be hard and fast. Other people might want to pee too, you know. Do you know what I mean?"

"Hard and fast." Taz's head bobbed up and down as he wiggled his ass to show his agreement with Reed's terms.

Reed focused on that tantalizing flesh, ignoring the lack of ambiance, as well as the fact that a plane full of people sat just on the other side of that door, too close for comfort. Gods, the things being in love made you do, although this one pretty well took the cake. Would he want it any other way? *Hell no!*

Problem number one: they weren't at home, and he didn't carry lube about on him, although perhaps in the future he might have to consider doing so. But that didn't help him any now, and he sure as hell wasn't about to plow a dry field. So, necessity being the damn mother of invention, and because it was quick and easy and worked better than nothing, he gathered all the saliva he could muster into his mouth and spit into his hand, rubbing the result over his erection, where it mingled with the precum already leaking from the head.

Was he really going to be this crazy, he kept asking himself even as he spread Taz's cheeks, not taking his usual pause to admire the view, praying that the ever-ready alien could handle this, as he plunged inside of him.

Taz emitted a loud bellow. At least it sounded that way to Reed's overly sensitive ears. In reality, it was more of a low purr. *Dear God, how thin are these walls? Oh to hell with it!*

He was pressed tightly against Taz's back as it was; there was just no room to maneuver there, no matter how you sliced it. Taz's ass was fairly reverberating, as if he was trying to suck Reed's dick in as far as he could.

Reed pulled out and pushed in again, producing another muted wail of approval. Taz's hands were spread-eagled against the wall, supporting his weight over the toilet. "I can't touch myself," he moaned. "Please, Reed?"

Reed wrapped his hand around Taz's dick and stroked him hard and fast. They really, *really* needed to get the hell out of there before they got busted. The last thing he wanted was to end up in trouble with the airline. They couldn't afford that, not with Taz being an alien. On that happy thought, he plowed into his lover.

"Come for me," Reed whispered as he filled Taz with his seed.

Five minutes later he hustled Taz out the damn door, back to his seat. A few minutes later, Reed walked out himself. One or two passengers glared at him, but no one was shouting and pointing. Well, one of the flight attendants gave him the hairy eyeball, but she didn't say anything. Surely that wasn't the first time they'd seen that happen on a flight?

Reed returned to his seat, and Taz rested his head against his shoulder, neither one of them saying much. The rest of the trip passed without incident—or any more sexcapades—and they managed to land with minimal fuss from Taz. He'd have to remember that the next time he wanted Taz to be more sedate—a sated Taz was a pliable Taz. Hurrying to the luggage carousel, Reed got their suitcases; then they picked up their car from the rental agency and were on their way.

An hour into the drive, Taz turned to Reed, a thoughtful expression clouding his eyes. "Are you okay? You've been really quiet."

Reed grasped Taz's hand, letting their interlinked fingers rest on the console. "I'm fine, babe. Just… you know. I guess it's finally hitting me about Dad and all. Plus, it's been a while since I saw the whole family."

"You miss them?"

"Yes, I do." Reed pursed his lips. "Well, I miss my parents, even if they do get on my nerves some. I miss my sister, Renee. I didn't tell you about her, did I? She's thirty-two, she's single, and she owns her own bar. She's great, and you're going to love her. She's sure to be crazy over you…."

"But?"

"Yeah, there's always a 'but,' isn't there?" Reed shook his head, his eyes never leaving the road. "The butt... and yes, I *am* talking about a certain part of the anatomy... is my brother, Jacob. At thirty-four, he's the oldest of us, and he's married and has a kid of his own."

"And what's the problem?"

"The problem is I'm gay. At least it's a problem for him. A very big problem. He thinks being gay is a choice, and a sin. Which is bad enough, but he's a bully too—he's mean. He picked on me when we were kids. Of course, once I got bigger and could stand up for myself, things got... heated. I wouldn't take his shit and I fought back."

"That's ridiculous!" Indignation laced Taz's voice. "No one should be forced to accept another's excrement...."

Reed tactfully tried not to explode with laughter, choking out, "No, that just means I wouldn't accept him giving me any trouble."

"Oh. Well, if he causes any trouble, I shall certainly set him straight." Taz nodded, pressing his lips together tightly. Reed tightened his grip on their joined hands.

"I'm so glad I have you, babe. Together, we can do anything." He didn't think there would be a problem with his mother letting them sleep together in her house. At least not from her. Jacob could go fuck himself, for all Reed cared. If it seemed like he'd make a stink about it for Mom, though, they'd go to a hotel. No way was he pretending they weren't together, or settling for separate but equal accommodations.

FOUR

THE TRIP to his parents' house was pleasant, the time passing quickly as he and Taz chatted. When they were still thirty miles away, he called his mom to let her know they were almost there. Before he felt ready, they were entering Hydethorne Hills Retirement Community. The community was arranged around the gently rolling hills of Lake Hydethorne, an assortment of small but nice-looking homes, all wearing the scrubbed Floridian look that seemed to be so popular—white stucco walls, flat roofs, and plenty of palm trees.

He'd just parked when his sister, Renee, came bouncing down the front steps. "Reed!"

"That's Renee," Reed informed Taz before he could ask. "Come on, let's get out and meet her before she pulls the car door off in her excitement. And I'm kidding. She can't really jerk the door off the—"

"I knew that. Humans aren't that strong." Taz grinned at Reed as he opened the driver's door.

"Reed! And oh my, who's this?" Renee bypassed her brother and hurried over to Taz's side of the car, jerking open the passenger door. "Well, hello there, handsome. Mom said my baby brother had a boyfriend, but she didn't say how cute he was. Nice to meet you,

I'm Renee. And I have to tell you, I want the name of whoever does your hair. I love those highlights."

"Whoever does—" Taz began.

Reed hastily interjected. "Nobody you know. Very exclusive." Better to let his sister think Taz went to an overly high-priced hair stylist than to suspect his calico mane was natural and not unusual where he came from.

Renee pouted, but only for a moment, as Taz unfolded himself from the interior of the vehicle. "Oh Reed, you really do know how to pick them." She gave Taz an admiring glance as she threaded her arm through his. "Let's go inside so Mom can meet you. She's gonna flip!"

"How's Mom doing?" Reed joined them, taking Taz's hand in his, gripping it tightly for security—his own, as much as Taz's. He was still feeling off-kilter from the news about his dad, although his common sense told him that since they were at the house, not the hospital, the situation couldn't be too dire.

"Pretty good, considering." Renee pulled them toward the house. "I had a hard time convincing her to come home and take a shower and get some rest. I reminded her you'd be here soon, so I think that did the trick. She wanted to be presentable to meet your boyfriend."

"What's the news on Dad? What do the doctors say?"

Before he could get a reply, the front door opened once again, and Jeanette Hatcher stood framed there, shading her eyes against the Florida sun as she looked out at them. For a brief moment, terrible thoughts coursed through Reed's brain, but at his mother's welcoming smile, he relaxed, allowing Renee to drag them up the steps. He almost felt as though he was back in kindergarten once more, being led into school after recess. It was good to come home again—literally, not figuratively.

Renee stepped to the side and pulled Taz with her, allowing Reed the first moment with his mother alone. He hugged her tightly, feeling for the first time how fragile she was, and the thought scared him. He'd never had to consider his parents' mortality before. He thrust those morbid thoughts aside.

"I'm so glad you came, Reed. I hated to bother you—" his mother murmured.

"Of course I came, don't be silly. I love you and Dad. I wouldn't want to be anywhere else." He kissed her softly on the cheek before turning to other matters. Managing to disengage Taz from Renee's clutches, he took his hand. "Mom, this is Taz." For a split second, he was concerned about Taz's reaction, but his fears proved to be groundless, as Taz impulsively threw his arms around Reed's mother and hugged her.

"Hello, Mom, I'm very happy to meet the mother of my wonderful Reed."

Reed heard Renee's giggle, felt his own cheeks warm, but in a good way, as his mother returned the hug, her eyes smiling at him over Taz's shoulder. He could see the love and approval there, and he felt his shoulders release some tension at the sight.

Thank God for Taz's natural good humor and warmth. He should have realized Taz would win over his mother instantly.

"Aren't you just the sweetest thing?" Jeanette patted Taz on the back while smiling up at Reed. She leaned closer, dropping her voice, although Reed could still hear her words. "I think you're going to be good for him. He works entirely too much. He needs to learn how to enjoy life again." She got very quiet. "You just never know when things will… change."

Taz squeezed her tightly, even as Reed wondered if he was missing his own mom. Assuming he had one. Well, everyone did. Still…. "You're talking about what happened with your mate, right? I hope everything turns out okay with that."

Jeanette frowned at Taz's choice of words, but she was too well-bred to make Taz uncomfortable by commenting on them. "That's exactly what I'm talking about. Live life while you can." Jeanette hugged Taz one last time and stepped back. She held her arms out to her youngest again.

Emotions flooded Reed's throat as he wrapped his mom in his arms and held on for dear life. Yes, there were times she got on his nerves with her endless chatter about his taking time off from work, coming back home, finding a steady man... but this was his mom. He bent down and rested his head on her shoulder. Taking a deep breath, he inhaled the scents so familiar from his childhood. She still smelled like warm vanilla and fresh baked bread. The sweet security of his mother's love calmed his racing heart and settled the worries he'd refused to let take root. He'd worked so hard to suppress his fears.

"I'm sorry, Mom," Reed whispered, fighting not to choke up. Those three words covered a wealth of things he was sorry for: not coming home sooner, not calling more often, moving so far away... the big gash in his father's favorite leather recliner that he blamed Renee for.

"It's okay, sweetie."

And just like that, all was forgiven. This was still one of the most important people in his life. The other lay on a hospital bed not far from there.

Jeanette patted Reed on the back one last time and released the death grip she had on her son. "Now, how about we grab something to eat? Some people from church brought dinners over. Anyone hungry?"

Taz rubbed his stomach. "I am very hungry," he admitted. "The food we got on the flying machine wasn't very satisfactory at all." He sniffed indignantly.

"It wasn't meant to be a meal, babe, just a snack." Reed forced himself not to laugh at Taz, who'd been decidedly unhappy with the assortment of nuts they'd received, in almost unopenable bags. He noticed his mom smile at Taz's statement. That would give her something to focus on, anyway. She'd always been a nurturer.

"Then come on in, honey, and let's feed you properly. Renee, you want to help me, please? Let these two get cleaned up? You can just throw your bags in one of the spare rooms. You have luggage, don't you?"

"Yes, Mom, we have luggage." Reed tugged on Taz's hand. "We'll be right in with it. And then we'll wash up," he hastily added, not needing a reminder and knowing how his mother's mind worked.

While the women headed to the kitchen, he and Taz got their suitcases from the trunk of the rental car and carried them inside, down the hall where the bedrooms were situated. The room at the end of the hall was the master suite; there were two rooms on the left side of the hall. He saw Renee's flowery suitcase beside the single bed in the smaller room, then realized she'd left the double in the room beside his parents to them. Good. They didn't have to stay at a motel. There was obviously room for him and Taz to be together.

The room they were to stay in was bright and airy, like the rest of the house. The bedspread was adorned in Shasta daisies, and the wallpaper mimicked them. A vase of fresh cut flowers sat on the dresser, filling the air with their scent.

"We can unpack later," he told Taz, before he pulled him into his arms and kissed him. "Thank you so much for coming with me. I don't know what I'd do without you."

"Don't worry. I don't intend to let you find out." Taz smirked as he drew Reed closer and slid his hand down to rub Reed's ass. Reed moaned.

"Oh babe, I wish we could, but we don't have time. Besides, we can't chance your stripes coming out, not now. Later. When we're alone. I promise."

"Promises, promises," Taz grumbled.

"'Sides, we're gonna eat now, remember?" Reed reminded him. That idea produced a smile. Just when Reed thought he was off the hook, the evil alien pressed against him, rubbing their cocks together, then stepped back with a shit-eating grin.

Oh lord, but Taz could be difficult at times.

"You bad little cat—you will pay for that, later. I promise *you*." Reed knew his voice was husky, but he couldn't help it. One touch from Taz and he was hard as stone. He rearranged his stiff dick. "Great, now we're both hard."

Taz grinned, his eyes twinkling. He reached out and untucked Reed's shirt, making sure to smooth the material down in front. "There you go."

Reed jerked back. "Good God, I am not going to sit down at my Mom's table with a raging hard-on. Behave, Taz."

Taz untucked his shirt too. "Where's the fun in that?"

"Oh heaven help me." Reed rolled his eyes. "Taz, seriously...."

Taz raised an eyebrow. "So does that mean I can't play with you under the table while we eat?" He snorted out a laugh at the horrified look on Reed's face. "I'm kidding, Reed."

Reed forced himself to take a deep breath. "It would serve you right if you pushed me over the edge and I threw you on the table and made a meal out of you." He hoped the threat would be sufficient to keep his kitty in line.

Wrong.

Taz purred softly. "I can handle it if you can."

"I can't win, can I?" Chuckling softly, Reed pulled Taz close and nipped his bottom lip. "Bad kitty. When we get home, I'll tie you to the kitchen table and dine on you then. How's that?"

"Something to look forward to," Taz purred.

Reed pulled Taz out of the bedroom and into the kitchen before the bad little kitty got his dick any harder. If that was even possible. His mom had several dishes laid out on the bar. "Mmm, I see some of my favorites."

"Just serve yourself, sweetie, buffet style."

"Wow, looks good, Mom." Renee handed plates to Taz and Reed. "Dig in, boys."

Reed went first so Taz would have some idea what to do. Once everyone had taken their places at the table, Jeanette served drinks. Reed had barely swallowed some of his sweet tea when he heard a door slam shut and footfalls march down the hall. Reed's shoulders stiffened.

"Reed?" Taz looked at his lover.

"Mom? I'm here. Sorry I'm late, but…. Who are you?" The newcomer stood in the doorway, blatantly staring at Taz.

Reed worked to keep his voice steady. "Jacob, this is Taz. Taz? This is my brother, Jacob."

"How do you do, Jacob?" Taz said politely.

Jacob's face turned red, and his eyes narrowed as he looked between Reed and Taz. "Are you serious? You brought your gay lover here at a time like this? Are you insane? How dare you sit"—Jacob waved his hand in Taz's direction—"*that* at our mother's table. Have you no respect for your own mother?"

Reed slammed his fist on the table, his temper spiking. He knew, just *knew* Jacob would say something vile about his being gay. "I am not in the mood to deal with *your* issues, Jacob. So listen up, you son of a—"

Renee glared at Jacob. "Oh good Lord, spare us your homophobic bullshit for once, please. It's getting old. Reed has every right to bring home whoever he wants."

Jacob turned on Renee. "Of course you *would* defend something so disgusting and unnatural. After all, you're a single woman running a bar. A bar, for God's sake. Instead of finding a good man and settling down and having children, like God intended—"

"Oh boy, stand back. It's going to hit the fan now." Reed shook his head.

Renee threw her napkin on the table and stood. "Find me a man? I don't need a man to take care of me. I do that all on my own, and do just fine, thank you. I don't want to be barefoot and pregnant like *your* wife. You, brother dear, can kiss my skinny white—"

"Tell 'em, sis." Reed smugly looked on.

"That's enough! Jacob, Renee, Reed—all three of you button it. Jacob, this is my home and I will allow who I wish in it. You don't have a say in that." Jeanette's voice crashed across the table, brooking no argument. "You are certainly entitled to your opinion on women's rights and homosexuality. You are not, however, entitled to come in my home and beat your brother and sister over the head with them. Either you keep a civil tongue in your head, or you may leave. I will not have a guest insulted. And at my own table, no less. You were taught better than that."

A flush covered Jacob's face. "Yes, Mama."

"Renee? Sit down, please. While I have no problem with what you do for a living, I do have a problem with profanity at my table. Kindly refrain from cussing around me."

Renee lowered her eyes. "Yes, Mama."

"And Reed, stop egging your sister on."

"Yes, Mama."

Finally Jeanette looked at Taz. "I'm sorry you had to be exposed to that, sweetie. They were taught manners, even if they don't always show them. You are very welcome here. Now, we will sit down and have a pleasant meal without any more derogatory remarks. Am I clear, Jacob?"

An uncomfortable silence ensued that stretched into what felt like forever, everyone frozen into a tableau of horror. At least, in Reed's eyes. He watched as Jacob's dark brows furrowed until there was only one thick brow across his forehead, his mouth pursing into a tight line, his nostrils flaring in impotent fury. Finally, he sneered at Reed, before turning to their mother. "Clear," he said tersely, nodding. But Reed felt the hollowness of his acquiescence.

He'd been so focused on Jacob he'd failed to notice that Taz had risen, thrown a protective arm before him, and was glaring at Jacob, not saying a word. Reed's heart swelled at the gesture, although he suspected that his brother could seriously damage his sweet little alien without half trying. Taz was built for heights and for speed and for impossible positions when they made love, but strength? Reed didn't think so. And he didn't want to find out.

"Jacob, sit down before you make Mom start twisting our ears as punishment. I'm too old for that now." That was Renee. Her words cut the tension in the room, at least as far as the others were concerned, producing smiles all around, and a titter from Taz, who'd taken his own seat and pushed it closer to Reed.

"How's Dad?" Jacob turned to Jeanette, ignoring Renee. She rolled her eyes at Reed and Taz behind his back, making rude gestures with her fingers. When Taz giggled loudly, Jacob whirled and glared, but by then, she was the epitome of innocence once more.

"Your father is resting comfortably. Once we eat, we can all go to the hospital and see him. Help yourself to what you see. Sweet tea's on the counter."

"Good." Jacob fixed a plate and took a seat at the table… as far away from Taz and Reed as he could get, although that wasn't very far, due to the size of the table. Silence blanketed the group again, the only sounds in the room the scrape of silverware against plates.

"So, Taz, what is it you do for a living?" Renee winked at Taz.

"I do the books for—"

"Really?" Jacob interrupted. "And your employer is okay with the fact you have all that hair? Must not be a very professional jobsite." Jacob waved his spoon at Taz.

"As a matter of fact, he works for me." Reed intercepted Jacob's question on behalf of his lover. "And as far as professional goes, would you like to know what I grossed last year? Bet it was more than you did. Besides, I happen to like his long hair."

Jacob snorted. "Figures. No one in his right mind—"

"Jacob Hatcher!"

Reed was grateful for his mother's stern admonition; it prevented him from the necessity of having to get in his brother's face for his callous words—the last place he actually wanted to be. The rest of the meal was eaten with a lack of conversation. Reed placed his hand on Taz's knee—as much to anchor himself as to reassure his lover. He was determined not to let Jacob get under his skin any more than he could help, although that was much easier said than done.

After everyone had eaten their fill, the leftovers were placed back in the fridge, and the dishes were rinsed and set into the dishwasher for later, once they'd returned from the hospital. A small argument ensued as to whose car to take, but they finally decided to split into two vehicles. One car seemed too small to hold both brothers. Besides, Reed could tell Jacob wasn't keen to have either him or Taz sit in his precious SUV. *So be it.*

In the interests of keeping peace, it was decided that Mom would ride with Jacob, while Renee would accompany Reed and Taz. Taz was very much taken with Reed's lively sister. He had no sisters himself, only an older brother. He was grateful that his brother, although prone to be orderly and disciplined in a military sort of way, was not an asshole like Jacob.

On the way to the hospital, Taz frequently turned in his seat to converse with Renee, who sat behind them. He told her the story of how he and Reed met—the truncated version, of course, leaving out any and all references to life in another galaxy, and traveling through space. She was enchanted and squealed constantly, playfully punching Reed in his shoulder.

"You two are soooo cute! And Taz is soooooo adorable! You guys gotta come to the bar and hang with me!"

"Of course!" Taz quickly replied. "We'd love to! How high will we be hanging?"

Reed quickly interjected before Renee had a chance to reply. "Ha-ha, funny. Taz. Great sense of humor." He hoped Renee was buying what he was selling.

Reed just shook his head as he followed Jacob off the interstate and to the hospital. He pulled in behind his brother and waited as Jacob entered the parking garage, tapping his fingers on the steering wheel. Of all the places Jacob could have chosen to park. Especially when there was outside parking available. But he knew damn well why his brother had chosen this route. Jacob moved through the gate and Reed pulled a ticket from the automatic dispenser. He followed Jacob to the fifth level and parked as close to the elevator as he could. His mom and Jacob waited there for them. The elevator opened to a glass crosswalk to another building. From there, they would take another elevator to the main floor of the hospital.

Reed didn't much care for the crosswalk, but Taz loved it. Reed had to nudge Taz along a couple of times. His lover kept stopping to watch the traffic that flowed under them. "This is neat," Taz whispered to Reed. They walked alone now, Renee having caught up with the others, probably to give them time to themselves.

"I guess so." Reed shrugged. "It's a little too high off the ground for me."

A grin crossed Taz's face. "This?" He waved at the glass hallway. "This is nothing, Reed."

"Still up off the ground," Reed mumbled.

Taz's eyes widened. "Are you afraid of heights?"

"Not really. It's just...." Reed blew out a breath and hurried Taz along. "The damn thing is made of glass. I mean... we're walking on glass. You can see straight down to the ground. And yeah, that freaks me out a bit."

"Oh." Taz bit his lip. He snagged Reed's hand. "It doesn't bother me. Then why are we on this thing if it makes you so uncomfortable? Why didn't we park on the ground?"

"Because Jacob knows I hate this glass crosswalk." Reed knew it really wasn't a good idea to be holding hands with another man in public, but he couldn't help himself. Just that connection to Taz calmed him, and he squeezed Taz's hand, seeking reassurance from his touch.

"Are you telling me he knew you didn't like this thing, but he still parked up here?" Taz glared at the back of Jacob's head. "What a horrible thing to do. I'm sorry, Reed, but your brother really is an asshole." Taz frowned.

Reed breathed a sigh of relief when they entered the hospital. He tightened his fingers around Taz's. Something sharp poked his hand. "Claws, kitten. And yes, he is."

They crossed the lobby and took another set of elevators up to the eighth floor where his dad's room was. The closer they got to the room, the tighter his chest became. Hospitals didn't really bother him, but he knew seeing his dad so helpless was going to turn his world upside down, shake his foundations in ways they'd never been shaken before.

Taz looked at Reed. "Are you okay?"

"Yeah. Just… you know. This isn't easy."

"I imagine not." Taz wrinkled his nose and leaned closer to Reed. "Do places like this always reek?"

Reed wanted to smack himself. He hadn't thought of Taz's sensitive nose. "Sorry, babe. I didn't think about the odor. What's it smell like to you? Hospitals always stink like antiseptic and cleaner and urine to me."

Taz rubbed at his nose and sniffed. "I smell that too, along with death and hopelessness."

Reed sighed. "I'm afraid that's all too often true. But not always. And not now, thank God. Come on, babe." Mom and Renee and Jacob were out of sight, probably in Dad's room. Just what he wanted—to make an entrance. It couldn't be helped, though. All he could hope was that Jacob hadn't already filled Dad's ear with his venom about him and Taz.

The room was a double, but the first bed was empty so, at least for now, his father had a private room. His mother sat in an armchair pulled up near the head of the bed, while Renee had planted her butt on the end of it. Jacob stood by the window, gazing at something, or nothing. Reed couldn't tell and didn't care. His focus was all on his father.

Herb Hatcher lay flat on his back, hooked up to machines on poles that flashed numbers and beeped to show they were operational. He looked small and pale in the standard-issue hospital gown. An IV sprouted from one arm. Reed followed the trail with his eyes to the stand it issued from. A bag of clear fluid hung at the other end. *Probably a saline drip*, he thought, his mind seizing on anything and everything to keep from acknowledging the truth: that his father was human and frail and would not live forever. A very uncomfortable thought.

"Hey kiddo," Dad greeted him with a smile, as Reed hastened to his unoccupied side, leading Taz, never dropping Taz's hand.

"Hi, Dad." Reed forced himself to be more chipper than he felt, although the almost normal tone in his dad's voice was a balm. Until this moment, he'd really feared the worst, but now it appeared to be better than he'd anticipated.

"Sorry for all the fuss. Making you come all the way from New York just because of some angina pains...."

"Don't be silly, Dad. And don't apologize. You didn't make me come. I wanted to make sure you were okay. I know it's been a while since I've been able to come down. I should apologize. You know, business...." That sounded lame even to him, but his dad never stopped smiling as Reed bent down and kissed his cheek before straightening once more.

He could see his dad's eyes move to Taz—was that a hint of a twinkle he saw there? His father's eyebrows rose questioningly, as his mother coughed, purposefully. Reed wished that Jacob wasn't there. This was not how he wanted to introduce his lover to his father. But this was the hand he'd been dealt.

He pulled Taz forward. "Dad, this is Taz." He fumbled for a moment, seeking the right word. Boyfriend sounded juvenile, lover sounded too racy, and significant other too politically correct. Before he could think of anything, Taz had leaned down and imitated Reed's kiss on his father's cheek.

"Hello, beloved father of my precious Reed!" he greeted him. "I am very happy to meet you, although I am sorry that you have been hurt. I wish you great felicitations and a long life...."

Jacob rolled his eyes. "Oh good God, where did you find this—"

Reed swung around to face Jacob and glared at him. "I'd advise you not to finish—"

"Jacob, I may be flat on my back in a hospital bed, but don't think because I'm not feeling well I'll put up with you acting like an ass." Herb's voice was weak, but the intent behind the words was quite clear. Satisfied he'd made his point, he clasped Taz's hand and smiled up at the young man that hovered over him. "Taz, it's nice meeting you. Sorry it had to be like this, but please know how happy

I am Reed brought you with him. I'm glad he didn't need to make that trip all alone."

"Oh, thank you!" Taz squeezed Herb's hand. "Reed and I are very pleased to have your blessing."

Reed favored Jacob with a death stare, then swung his arm around Taz as he turned to face his dad. "Never had any doubt how Mom and Dad would react, Taz. Dad's right, though. It was easier having you with me. Even if the trip down did bother you some."

Taz grinned up at Reed. "You helped keep my mind off how dangerous these planes of yours are."

"Oh? Afraid of flying, Taz?" Herb asked. "Reed's mother doesn't care for it either."

"Yes, well...." Reed knew he'd wrap his tongue around his head and strangle himself with it before he told his dad just how 'helpful' he'd been to Taz on the way down in order to overcome that so-called fear of flying. What his dad didn't know wouldn't send him into a real heart attack. "They give you any idea of how long it's gonna be before they spring you?"

Herb huffed out a breath. "A day or two, at least. They want to monitor me for a bit longer and try me on some different meds."

Jeanette raised an eyebrow at Herb. "And discuss a change in your diet too."

"Bah," Herb grumbled. "And humbug. Damn doctors."

"I sure don't envy you, Mom," Renee added. "He's going to be hard to handle, isn't he?"

Jeanette gave a delicate snort. "If that's what you think, you don't know your old mama very well." She gave her husband a meaningful glance and he groaned.

Reed felt a weight lift at the normal family banter. That sounded more like his dad. The old man really was going to be okay. For the first time since he got the call, he relaxed. He'd had no idea how tense he'd been. He leaned against Taz gratefully, exhaling with relief.

"Can't you save that stuff for somewhere else?" That was Jacob again, naturally.

Before Reed could reply, Renee had fired off a response. "Is it all PDA that disturb you or just gay ones? Are you afraid of seeing happy people because it reminds you of how joyless your life is?"

"No, it reminds me that my brother's a flaming homo—"

"Enough!" Jeanette's voice cracked like a whip. She pointed her finger at her oldest son. "If you can't act civilized, then you can leave. Right now. Do you understand me?"

Jacob's face flamed as he glowered at Reed and Taz. He looked as if he were in danger of having a heart attack.

"Your brother doesn't seem well, Reed," Taz ingenuously observed. "Do you think he needs a hospital room for himself?"

Reed tried not to snicker, but Renee guffawed, and both of Reed's parents smiled.

"Son...." Her voice softened, despite the fact that her oldest was acting like an asshole. "Please...."

"I'm going to get something to drink. I'll be back." Jacob glared at Reed, Taz, and Renee, and it was easy to see that he was willing them to be gone before he returned. Especially Taz. Without a word, he turned and stomped down the hall.

"Wow, he should have that stick removed while he's here," Renee commented.

"Stick?" Taz quickly looked in the direction of the disappearing grump. "I still don't see any—"

The tension that Jacob had wrought was quickly eased by the round of loving laughter that filled the room. Reed kissed Taz softly. "It's just an expression, babe. Don't worry, I'll find that book somewhere. I promise."

FIVE

GOOD-BYES WERE said after Reed noticed his dad smothering yawns. His mom wasn't ready to leave, so she stayed behind with Jacob, who was still sulking in the waiting room. Renee decided to leave with Reed and Taz. Hugs were exchanged with the promise to return the next day. Not much was said as Renee followed Taz and Reed back to his car.

As they drove away from the hospital, Reed glanced into the rearview mirror and caught Renee's gaze. "Don't know about you, but I'm not ready to go home. Any suggestions?"

Renee shrugged. "I'm not either. Is anyone hungry?"

Taz folded one of his legs under him, infusing the action with more grace than Reed would have thought possible in a compact car, and faced Reed. "Well, a little. I could wait, though, if no one else is ready to eat."

Reed pulled up to a stop sign and actually paused, instead of his usual rolling stop, using the moment to glance at Taz with an apologetic look. "Visiting the hospital kind of left my stomach in knots. How about we just drive around, then we can eat. That okay with you, babe?"

"Sure. I'd like to see your family's home place. I've... ah, never been down here before." Taz carefully danced around the truth, careful not to say too much in front of Reed's sister. "This is much different from New York."

"Oh God, Reed. Don't tell me you've gone and hooked up with a Yank." Renee snorted, then reached across the seat and swatted Taz on the shoulder. "Welcome to the South, honey. We're not as backwoods as you've heard."

At Taz's confused expression, Reed hastily explained. "Backwoods just means someone who's not used to living in the city or around civilized people very much."

Taz winked at Reed as they pulled through the intersection. "Oh, I've seen backwoods and this isn't it. You should see—"

"Jesus Christ, when did they put in a Walmart?" Reed stepped over his lover's words and frowned at Taz in warning. "Last time I was here, this was all woods. And where did the old Sonic go?"

Renee readjusted her seat belt. "I hate these things. All they're good for is squashing my boobs and who needs that? Anyway, about the store. Thought you knew. We fought the Walmart coming in, not that it did any good. They're here, as you can see. As for the drive-in, they just tore down the old Sonic and moved across town to a bigger location. I've heard they plan to build something else where it was. Maybe an AutoZone."

"I'd forgotten how much you used to whine, when we were kids, about the damn seat belts." Reed grinned as Renee continued to fuss with the belt that stretched across her chest. Reed turned to Taz. "Mom had her hands full trying to keep that one buckled in. But yeah, now that you mention it, Renee, I can see that this place is really growing. It's surprising how much can change in just over a year, since my last visit."

Renee huffed. "Mom only caught me unbuckled because *someone*"—Renee glared at Reed in the front seat—"told on me. And maybe if you came home more than once in a blue moon...."

Reed clutched the steering wheel, a pang of guilt tearing through him. "I know, okay, Renee. I'm sorry about that. More sorry than you know."

Taz patted Reed reassuringly on the thigh and frowned his disapproval at Renee.

Renee leaned back against the headrest and blew out a deep breath. "Damn, didn't mean to go all Jacob-like on you. One bitch in the family's more than enough, isn't it? Just ignore me. I guess I'm still a little uptight. Sorry, Reed."

Reed loosened his stranglehold on the steering wheel. "Tell you what, buy me a drink, and I won't boot your ass out here in the middle of Main Street."

"You got a deal. We can grab a bite to eat too." Renee looked at Taz. "How'd you like to see my bar, Forever in Blue Jeans?"

Taz looked uneasily from Reed to Renee. "Um…." It was hard for him to follow their volatile mood changes.

Reed took Taz's hand. "It's okay, babe. Renee and I sometimes disagree. It's not the same like what you saw between me and Jacob."

Renee rolled her eyes. "Gawd no. I can *be* bitchy, Jacob *is* a bitch. Big difference."

Taz squeezed Reed's hand in return. "I understand. And I'd love to see your bar, Renee. Do we need to wear blue jeans to get in?"

Renee laughed. "You're so cute!" Reaching for Taz's braid, she fingered it gently before answering the question. "No, but I bet you look hot in them."

"Hey, mind not hitting on my boyfriend?" Reed glanced at her through the rearview mirror, but he was smiling beneath his jest.

"I don't mind hitting on him at all," Renee returned, sticking out her tongue. "You just be careful or I'll steal him away from you, Reed Hatcher!"

"Oh no, I cannot be stolen from Reed," Taz protested. Reed knew only too well that Taz was thinking of Vorlod and what had happened to him.

"She wouldn't really. Don't worry, babe. She's just being funny."

"Oh, okay." A trace of doubt lingered in Taz's voice. He wanted to move closer to Reed, but the console between them interfered with this idea, so he contented himself with holding Reed's hand tightly.

Renee gave Reed the directions, and it wasn't long before they'd arrived at Forever in Blue Jeans. Reed locked the rental car, slid the key into his pocket, and reached for Taz. The bar sat at the end of a small strip mall in a modest business district. Reed knew his sister had been working on her newly acquired establishment, erasing all trace of the previous owners and making it her own, slowly but surely. He was excited to see what she'd done so far.

The outside was low-key, nothing flashy or gaudy, except for the neon lights that blinked in the front window, courtesy of various local beer distributors. He knew they were freebies and, as his sister had explained, if you wanted to do business with them, it came with the territory. Plus, it was good advertising and helped to draw in thirsty passersby.

When they reached the front door, Renee held it for them. "Welcome to Forever in Blue Jeans," she said, pride obvious in her voice. "Come on in."

The back wall was composed of beautiful exposed brick behind a long counter that acted as the bar. Padded high-back chairs were positioned down the expanse, and the wood surface gleamed with age and care. Pictures, plaques, beat-up street signs, old movie posters, the occasional gilded mirror, and other knickknacks were hung on the brick wall. A big screen TV held a place of honor, showing a previously aired football game. Shelves in the same wood grain as the bar held an assortment of liquor and glasses, highlighted by spotlights in the ceiling.

Several tables were placed throughout the room, and there were booths along another wall with more televisions playing different programs. More neon signs flashed around the room and one corner held a state-of-the-art jukebox. Huge beams crossed the ceiling, the wood stained to match the bar. Ceiling fans turned lazily, stirring the air as people sat and talked or watched TV.

Reed followed Renee in, noting the place was half full. She led them through the throng of tables toward a booth in the back, away from most of the crowd. Several people spoke to her as they wound through the customers, and Renee stopped to talk to each and every person, taking time to introduce her brother and his boyfriend. Reed was a little uncomfortable the first time she introduced them as a couple, but when not one person raised an eyebrow or frowned in disapproval, he felt better and began to relax. Taz, on the other hand, greeted everyone happily, taking great pride in being known as Reed's other half. An attitude Reed vowed to adopt for himself. Societal norms must be different on Taz's home planet, he thought wistfully, wondering if Earth would ever become so enlightened.

"Nice place you have here." Reed let Taz move into the booth first, then slid in next to him. He took Taz's hand and gripped it beneath the cover of the table. A waitress brought them a menu and took their drink order.

"It feels… pleasant," Taz commented, as he read through the menu that sat between them once the waitress left. "It's different than the places we go to at home."

Renee snorted. "This isn't New York, Taz. We're different down here… more laid-back."

The waitress brought three cold beers and took their food orders.

"It's really looking good," Reed complimented his sister as he glanced around. He admired Renee for her willingness to work hard for what she wanted and for her strength in dealing with difficult situations. He wasn't as brave as she was in that respect. He preferred to avoid conflict, whereas Renee generally took the bull by the horns and said bring it on.

"Thanks, bro. It is coming along, if I do say so myself."

"Business seems good."

"Yeah, no complaints. I guess people find money to drink with even in the bad times, eh?"

Reed nodded. "Isn't that the truth?"

This was a far cry from the bars that Reed had taken Taz to in New York. Those were what Reed liked to call trendy. Or upscale, even. They had a faster pulse, a more rapid heartbeat, and the people dressed more in suits and fancier clothes. These people were not so dressed up, and yet Taz felt at home here with Reed and Renee.

He squeezed Reed's hand, moving their joined grasp to a not very subtle position over Reed's crotch. Reed raised an eyebrow and moved it a bit to the left. Taz only grinned.

"What's the smile for?" Renee leaned toward them, almost knocking her beer over in the process. She scooted it to the side for safekeeping.

"I'm happy," Taz announced. "Very, very happy." He slid as close to Reed as he could, which earned a squeal from Renee.

"Wow, you sure know how to pick 'em, Reed. Hey, Taz, got a brother?"

Reed wasn't taking any chances. Before Taz could explain anything about his family tree, he diverted his attention in another direction. "Oh look, a jukebox," he exclaimed, as if he'd just discovered the thing existed. "Let's go see what's on the hit parade, shall we?" He pulled Taz out of the booth before he could ask him why a parade needed to be hit; he could just hear the question forming now. "Be right back," he told Renee, guiding Taz carefully.

Taz oohed and aahed as he ran his hand over the brightly lit surface. "Ah, an automated music-playing device that's usually coin-operated." Sometimes he sounded like he swallowed an intergalactic guide to Earth culture. Other times, the man was clueless.

"That's one way of saying it." Reed fished some money out of his pocket while he looked over the selection. "Hmm, how about this song? It's got a good beat." No use asking Taz for suggestions. No way he'd know any of the titles.

The music belted out and spread through the room. Taz nodded his head to the rhythm, toes tapping, hips gyrating in small circles. When he couldn't stand it anymore, he turned to Reed. "Let's dance!"

"I, ah… I—oh boy." Reed dragged his hands through his hair. "Babe, there's not a dance floor here. It's not like the places we went to at home. This music's just to listen to, not dance to."

Taz's lower lip stuck out. "Where's the fun of that?" He glanced around the room, his eyes falling on the long bar as a mischievous look crossed his face. "Well, if there's not a dance floor, then I guess we'll just have to make do, huh?" Taz winked and walked away from Reed.

Reed hurried after his retreating boyfriend. It didn't take a genius to figure out where Taz was going. And what his intentions were. "Oh shit, Taz, you're not really going to—"

That was as far as he got. Up Taz went, his movements graceful as he leapt onto the bar. Several people moved out of the way while Reed stood there, his mouth hanging open. Taz's hands fastened onto his belt loops, as he stomped to the beat of the music, as if he'd been doing this all his life. For all Reed knew, maybe he had.

"Oh. My. God." Reed forced himself to breathe. There was no doubt his guy looked sexy up there, but he didn't think Renee wanted them to do stuff like that. Not here. Jeez, he needed to do something, and damn quickly. But before he could open his mouth or speak another word, one of the bartenders jumped up next to Taz, and then they were both of them boot scooting on the bar. Well, Taz *would* have been if he had boots on, but he was still doing a fine job of it. Watching them, Reed prayed that the finish on the bar wasn't an expensive one as they were surely going to ruin it at this rate.

"Well, I'll be damned." Renee joined Reed; she sounded as surprised as he felt.

"Oh hell, Renee, I'm so sorry." Time to end this before it got any worse. Reed stepped toward the bar just as another one of Renee's people hopped up and joined the dancing twosome. Others clapped and called out encouragement, while Reed wondered how the hell he was going to get his kitten down from his perch.

"Sorry?" Renee slapped Reed on the arm. "Are you kidding me? Just look at them. My customers are having a good time, my staff is having a good time—hell, *I'm* going to have a good time!"

Reed's mouth hit the floor again as Renee clambered up and joined them on the bar. Good Lord, what had his lover started? When Taz held his hand out, Reed just shook his head frantically. He wasn't the type to do stuff like that; he just wasn't brave enough. More than likely, he'd just look silly. He was content to watch from the sidelines, enjoy the show.

He really should've known better. How long had they been together now?

Before he had time to react, someone pushed him from behind and both Taz and Renee were pulling him onto the bar, despite him complaining all the way. All he could do was follow their lead and hope he didn't look too ridiculous. Someone else was feeding the jukebox now, and the hits just kept on coming. Luckily, before things got too carried away, a slow number popped up in the middle of all the toe-tapping selections. Reed took advantage of the lull to finagle Taz off the bar, promising him something special if he cooperated, although he was careful to leave his wording loose. He'd worry about delivering on that promise once he caught his breath. Maybe Taz would forget about it once they got their food.

And speak of the devil, there it was now, praise the Lord. That would keep Taz's attention. At least for a few minutes.

They'd ordered one appetizer sampler for the table, a three-tiered lazy Susan that contained sliders and chicken wings, loaded potato skins and fried cheese, along with an assortment of dips. It was meant for as many as six people to enjoy, but with Taz there, Reed suspected there'd be no leftovers. Although, to be honest, he and his sister were consuming their fair share of the tasty comestibles.

"Man, this is really good," Reed mumbled around a chicken wing.

Taz giggled at the sight of sauce decorating the corner of Reed's lips. He reached his finger out and wiped it off as Reed set the picked-clean bone onto his plate. Before he could grab another, Taz took Reed's hand, and inserted one finger between his own lips, sucking at the sauce. He was gratified to see the expression of complete surprise that overtook Reed, his eyes growing wider as he continued to suck at Reed's finger, mimicking the fellatio he enjoyed so well. He thought that was a pretty word to describe one of his favorite activities with Reed, whether he was giving or receiving.

"Um, um, um… Taz," Reed mumbled, but Taz noticed he made no move to remove his finger. He thought he heard Renee giggle, but his focus was on Reed. Nothing else mattered. When he finally pulled Reed's finger out, it was just to ask where the men's room was. Renee pointed across the room.

"Over there. Say, those are some cool tattoos.…"

They were up and gone before Renee could finish her thought.

"Taz, what in the—"

Taz didn't respond, dragging Reed through the empty men's room to the farthest stall from the door, which was also the largest. He pushed him inside, closed the door, and pressed Reed up against it, taking his mouth in a passionate kiss, even as he ground against him needily. His hand was already at Reed's belt, blithely unbuckling it. When he came up for the air he suspected Reed needed more than he did—as his lung capacity was pretty good—he dropped to his knees and unzipped Reed.

"Taz, wait… no… Taz… ohmigod… here? Really?" Reed braced himself against the door, his body trembling, as Taz pulled his pants out of the way, bringing his cock out into the open and swallowing it whole. "Oh shit, son… shit fire… shit shit shit.…" The mumbling grew more mangled as Reed tangled his hands in Taz's hair and clenched.

Taz loved the taste of Reed, and he saw no reason why he could not enjoy him wherever they were. He'd remembered to be discreet, hadn't he? Not in front of other people. That was one of Reed's cardinal rules. Taz loved to make Reed feel good, loved his reactions when he touched him, and loved to be touched by him. He loved *Reed.*

Pulling back, he placed little teasing kisses on the head of Reed's cock, savoring the salty sweet fluid that dribbled from the slit. He regretted the fact that they had limited space to maneuver in this place. He'd love nothing better than to slide one or two fingers inside of Reed, adding to the pleasure he offered his lover. Maybe later, once they returned to Reed's family home.

"Oh God, babe, hurry," Reed frantically hissed. "We shouldn't be doing this here. What if someone complains?"

"Let them," Taz answered, licking the hard, throbbing shaft in front of him.

"It's dangerous." Reed moaned when Taz flicked the head of his cock. "Your stripes are showing too. Even Renee noticed. We can't take chances like this."

Taz looked up at Reed, some of the joy leaving his face. "I just wanted to make you feel good. I'm sorry, Reed."

Reed tilted Taz's head back so he could see his eyes. "Oh sweetheart, don't look like that. I'm just trying to keep you safe. If something happened to you...."

"I'll be fast," Taz promised and leaned back over Reed's dick, his head bobbing up and down.

"So good, so good," Reed groaned. "Tonight, I promise tonight I'll take care of you."

Taz let Reed's dick hit the back of this throat, and the muffled grunt above him warned that his lover was about to come. He barely managed to pull off enough to taste Reed. Swallowing frantically, he gulped down all Reed had to give. Several little kitten licks later, he had Reed cleaned up and tucked safely back in his jeans.

REED PULLED Taz to his feet and held him close. He wanted to take the time to finish Taz off, but he didn't dare. They'd already spent too much time in here, and Taz's stripes were finally fading. He wasn't worried about the heckling he'd get from Renee, but what if someone had caught them and pitched a fit? God help them, what if Taz had been seen—if someone noticed his stripes? And hell, he hadn't even thought about his tail.

Reed whispered in Taz's ear. "You probably think I'm being an ass, but when we're together intimately like this, it has to be somewhere safe. You can't be seen, Taz, not while you're aroused. I wish it didn't have to be this way. Hell, I shouldn't even be saying things like this—not here. Do you understand what I mean?"

Taz nodded his head. "I do. I didn't think. I'm not used to hiding—"

"I know, babe. But you have to think about things like this. We both do." Reed smoothed Taz's hair before he stepped back and opened the door. "Ready to go back?"

"Yes." Taz looked down at the floor. "I'll try to behave."

Hearing what Taz said, Reed stopped and turned to face his lover. "Hey now, I love you the way you are, babe. I'm not asking you to be something you're not. I just want you to be careful. You brighten my life, and I don't want to lose the spark you've brought into it. Being careful doesn't mean you can't be you."

"Thank you." Taz's grin lit his face.

Reed quickly kissed Taz. "Come on, kitten, let's get back out there before Renee comes looking for us. And get ready, she'll have plenty to say about this little side trip we took."

"Will she be upset?" Taz chewed his lip as Reed pulled him along.

"Upset?" Reed pushed the door to the restroom open. "I doubt it. That's not to say we won't be the butt of several jokes when we get back to the table. So prepare yourself, and keep in mind she's just teasing. Even if I threaten to kill her, I'm just teasing too, okay?"

Reed and Taz returned to the table, and there sat Renee, waiting, with a huge shit-eating grin on her face. Reed let Taz slide in the booth first, then sat down next to him. He nonchalantly picked up a chip and dipped it.

"My baby brother, the exhibitionist."

"Shut up, Renee."

"I had to actually stop two of my waitresses from going in there. They wanted to see some man-on-man loving."

"Shut *up*, Renee." Reed picked up his drink and took a sip.

Renee leaned back against the booth. "So, do I have a huge mess to clean up in there?"

"I didn't spill a drop, so no mess," Taz volunteered.

Reed nearly spewed beer across the table. "Jesus H. Christ, babe!"

Renee laughed hysterically. "Oh, Taz, you are priceless."

Reed practically had to drag Taz from the bar. Truth be told, he was reluctant to depart himself. The time spent catching up with his boisterous older sister had been invaluable. Even though this place had never been his home, he found himself homesick for his family. Except for Jacob. He didn't think he could ever come to miss that asshole. But it *was* getting late, Renee *did* have a business to run, and he wanted to make sure his mother was taken care of. He'd decided that he'd cook dinner for her. Hopefully, Jacob would have other things to do. He didn't relish spending an evening with his brother, although he'd suffer his presence for his mother's sake, if he had to.

Renee insisted on walking them out. They'd just gained the sidewalk when Reed realized he'd forgotten something as the sun hit him square in the eyes. "Be right back, babe. Just be a second. Forgot my sunglasses." He kissed Taz gently on the lips. Not waiting for a response, he pushed open the door to the bar and hadn't taken more than a few steps when he ran smack dab into someone.

"Damn, I'm sorry," he apologized, his hands automatically clutching at the other for balance.

"Don't be sorry, Reed." An all-too familiar deep voice resounded in his ears. One he'd hoped to never hear again. With growing apprehension, he raised his eyes. Yep, it was him. Peyton Wheeler. Ex-lover and complete asshole. Six foot two, hair so black it was almost blue, well-styled in an expensive businessman's special, eyes a deep sapphire blue, and a cleft in his chin that men and women alike drooled over. But the exterior of a model hid a wealth of sins and an appalling personality. He was a control freak extraordinaire.

So what the hell was he doing here in Lake Hydethorne? And did Reed even want to know?

He clamped down on himself, on his body's almost automatic inclination to servility. Peyton was nothing to him, and he didn't have to listen to him. Ever again. He took a deep breath and tried to skirt the mountain of man, releasing his arms as soon as he recognized the voice. Unfortunately, Peyton had not done the same, which made getting around him difficult.

"Excuse me," he mumbled. "I just need to get something." He glanced toward the table where they'd been sitting. It was already cleared, and his sunglasses were nowhere in sight. Damn.

"What's the rush? I haven't seen you in such a long time. I mean, you just up and moved north. Why not join me and we can get caught up?"

Reed took a breath, trying to control his rapidly beating heart, his shoulders hunching. Get caught up? The last thing he wanted to do was get caught up with Peyton, now or ever. What would they get caught up *on*? The fact that Peyton had mentally abused him? Slapped him a few times? Treated him like a slave? Or the fact that Reed *let* him? Oh wait, they could talk about how he just jumped up and moved clear across the country to get away from the asshole.

"Reed? Did you hear me?" Peyton shook his head. "I swear, some things never change. Still can't make a decision without help, can you?"

Reed flinched when Peyton's fingers tightened on his arm. Fuck, he knew that tone of voice, and he cringed at the memory. Besides, what he said wasn't true. He *could* make decisions. He made them every day for his business—his business that was doing very well. At that thought, Reed stiffened his spine. Hadn't Peyton told him time and again he was too stupid to run his own business? According to his ex, the only reason he got his teaching certification was because he went into Elementary Education. He'd wanted to teach Kindergarten. Peyton called that glorified babysitting, nothing more, said that was why Reed could do it. Reed and any other chimp with half a brain.

Reed jerked his arm back. "Get caught up? Why in the hell would I want to do that? Let me make this totally clear: I'd rather swim in alligator-infested waters than sit down and spend even a second getting caught up with you. Now get the hell out of my way, I'm leaving."

"Still got that smart mouth, I see." Peyton leaned closer, eyes narrowed. "You'd think you'd learn—"

"Reed? What's the holdup? Couldn't you find your—oh, hey Peyton." Renee patted Reed on the back.

"No, the table was cleared." Reed clenched his fist, carefully hiding it alongside his leg. "You know Peyton?"

"I do, indeed." Renee smiled at Reed's ex. "He's one of my best customers. Imagine my surprise when he walked in here shortly after I opened."

Reed felt sick. Peyton had moved here that long ago? Why?

"The job moved me down to Lake Hydethorne about a year after your parents moved here." Peyton's lips twitched, almost as if he knew what Reed was thinking. "It was nice running into people I knew from home. Made the move much easier."

Reed wouldn't know about that. He'd been all alone in New York.

"We need to get going—I left Taz in the car. One of the wait staff probably picked your sunglasses up and dropped them in the Lost and Found behind the bar. I'll go get them." Renee smiled at Peyton. "Oh yeah, Dad got your card too. Thanks, that was nice."

Reed waited until Renee flounced off to vocalize his disturbance. "What the fuck are you doing? You know my family never knew we dated. You didn't want them to know. So why are you buddying up with them?"

"You're overreacting. As usual. I happened to move down here, and then I ran into your sister. Nothing more." Peyton grinned at Reed, but his complacent smile was too much of a smirk for Reed's taste. "So what if I got to be friends with them? By the way, who is Taz?"

"No one you need to be concerned about," Reed hissed. Renee was already walking back to them, dangling his glasses from one hand. "Stay away from me, Peyton. I mean it."

Peyton's face closed up, the sunny smile gone. "You don't tell me what to do. Thought you'd have learned that by now."

"Fuck off."

"Here you go." Renee held out Reed's glasses. "See you later, Peyton. Maybe we can all get together before Reed goes back to New York."

"Oh, definitely. Just say when. You and Jacob have my cell, right?"

The smile on Peyton's lips made Reed want to throw a table at the bastard. He'd exchanged numbers with his family? What the hell?

"Yup. One of us will give you a call. Come on, Reed. Something tells me leaving Taz this long in the car might not be a good idea."

That, and only that, was the reason why he finally moved. Leaving Taz to his own devices did not sound like a good idea at all; he had to concur with his sister. Sure enough, by the time they got outside, they found Taz standing outside the window, staring with fascination at the assorted neon lights.

SIX

TAZ HAD gotten bored, waiting for Reed, especially after Renee had disappeared inside the bar too. He wished he'd gone with them. He liked Renee's bar. The people were friendly, and the food was good. And dancing with her and Reed had been great fun. A smile crossed his face at the memory. Letting himself out of Reed's rental, he dance-stepped his way onto the sidewalk, practicing some of the moves they'd done on top of the bar. That had drawn him a few glances from people passing by, equally divided between stares and smiles. Taz had returned the smiles, ignored the stares.

Then his attention was caught by the pretty lights in the bar's window, brightly colored words that spelled out various names. As he watched, some of them blinked on and off with reckless abandon, reminding him of the lights he'd seen from the top of the Empire State Building, where he'd first met Reed. The very thought made him ache for Reed all the more. Just then, he saw Reed come out of the bar, and he stretched his wiry frame and bounced up to his lover.

"Did you find what you were looking for?"

"Um, yeah. Got them."

For some reason, Reed seemed disturbed, and Taz frowned. He hated to see Reed upset, and it was clear to him that his previous good mood had entirely dissipated in the short time he'd been back inside the bar. "What's wrong, Reed?"

He watched as Reed forced a smile onto his face, but Taz could see it wasn't his usual natural smile. "Nothing, babe, everything's fine. Why don't we—" Whatever he might have been about to say was bitten off, as his head snapped toward something, or someone, behind him.

Taz turned to look. A tall dark-haired man approached. Instantly, Taz felt the hairs on the back of his neck rise, and he could feel his claws lengthen slightly as he assumed a defensive posture. There was something cold in the stranger's eyes, something off-putting, and Taz fell into instant dislike of him, whoever he was. He stepped automatically in front of Reed without thinking about what he was doing, obeying his own instincts. The man seemed surprised, and then taken aback by Taz's gesture.

"You following us now, Peyton?" Renee giggled, then punched the man's arm, a move that did nothing to allay Taz's apprehension. "Just kidding."

"I just had an idea," the man called Peyton said in a voice that seemed too smooth to Taz's ears, too unnatural. "I thought maybe we could go to the hospital together to see Herb, take him some flowers or something. Wouldn't that be cozy?"

Renee turned toward Reed. "That makes sense. Didn't you want to talk to Mom about coming home for dinner? Maybe Peyton can join us?"

Taz felt Reed's disturbance grow deeper, not by anything he said, but Taz knew. He just knew. He reached for Reed's hand and held it tightly, without words, his eyes never leaving the newcomer who stared back at him with what might have been simple curiosity—or hatred.

"Well, well, who's this?" Now it was the man's turn to pretend to smile, but Taz saw through his phoniness, even if he didn't know why he was shamming. "Are you babysitting, Reed?"

Taz felt the tension in Reed's arm, but before his lover could answer, Taz had responded. "No, he's not babysitting. We don't have any children. Yet."

That stopped conversation real quickly, as three heads turned toward Taz, who stood his ground, eyes riveted on what he perceived to be a threat to his Reed.

Renee was the first to break the strange silence. "Well, hey, why don't you and Taz go work on that? I'll go to the hospital with Peyton, and we'll bring Mom home and all have supper, how does that sound?"

"So this is Taz, is it?"

Taz didn't like the way this man said his name, but he was too polite to get into an altercation with someone Renee obviously liked. He had manners, after all, and that would be rude. But he couldn't help but wish this Peyton person weren't there. He had brought a disturbance into their lives, and Taz just wanted him to go away. Now.

"Come on, Taz," Reed mumbled, pulling him along.

Once they were in the car and buckled in, Taz looked at Reed. His lover's lips were pinched, jaw set tight, and his nostrils were flared. Taz couldn't remember the last time he'd seen Reed this upset, and that upset him. Usually Reed was calm and easygoing, but not right now. His whole demeanor shouted unease, and he looked like he wanted to hit something… or maybe drive straight back to New York. The grip he had on the steering wheel left his knuckles white with strain.

"Who was that?" Taz asked quietly. They needed to talk about this before Reed broke that thing he used to control this machine.

"No one worth mentioning, believe me," Reed snapped.

"Reed…."

Reed clenched the steering wheel again, then blew out a breath. "Sorry, babe. Jesus, I didn't mean to snap at you. Long story short, he's an old boyfriend. When we dated, he was in the closet, so no one knew we were seeing each other. That includes my family. And thank God they didn't."

Taz watched the way Reed's hands tightened and untightened on the wheel. Reed's body was as stiff as a Malgar tick after it fed… the nasty things. "And…? There's more to this than that. He makes you very uncomfortable, I can tell."

Another deep breath sounded from the driver's seat. Taz reached over, pried one of Reed's hands off the steering wheel, and rubbed it against his cheek. "I love you, you know that. You can tell me anything."

"Aw God, Taz. I was young and stupid. The fact he didn't want anyone to know he was screwing me should've told me something, but I didn't listen. But that wasn't the worst of it." Reed squeezed Taz's hand. "He talked to me like I didn't have enough sense to come in out of the rain." Reed shook his head. "What I mean is he talked to me like I was stupid. He belittled me and...."

"And...?"

"Fuck. He even went so far as to hit me a few times. Just openhanded slaps, no fists but, after the third time, I'd had enough and—"

"By the stars, he *hit* you?" Taz actually growled, the sound low and menacing.

Reed took his eyes off the road for a second and glanced at Taz. "Easy with the claws, babe."

"Oh, oh, I'm so sorry! I didn't mean to—He hit you? That makes me want to.... Wait a minute." Taz's eyes widened. "You said he was screwing you? But I thought you didn't really like to bottom?"

"Yeah. He's the reason I haven't bottomed until you. Look, I'm going to swing into this fast food joint and grab a bucket of chicken and some side items. It'll have to do for dinner. I just don't feel like cooking right now." Reed pulled into line, craning his neck to see how far it went, not that it really mattered. Luckily not too far. "This is hard for me, Taz. Hard to look back at that time and see how much of a fool I was. But, yeah, I was on the receiving end of things. Plus, he's a control freak and nothing, *nothing* I did was good enough. And when it wasn't good enough, he sure let me know. And usually in the most hateful way possible."

"I am... I am so sorry, Reed. Even on my planet that's called abuse."

"You're right. It just took me a while to see that." Reed moved up in line, and placed the order. After he rolled up the window, he turned back to Taz. "So, when I finally got my head on straight, I broke up with him. Things really got hot and nasty then. That time, when he swung at me, I fucking swung back. Surprised him, let me tell you, but that was just the beginning. For the next month, he stalked me. Followed me everywhere. Did things. Creepy things. It got so bad, I moved to New York, just to get away from him."

"What did he do?" Taz laid their joined hands down on Reed's thigh.

"Well, I can't prove anything, and I don't know for sure he did these things, but I'm pretty sure it had to be him. My tires were slashed, all the plants on my front patio at my apartment were torn out of their pots, a brick was thrown through my bedroom window, the word fag was painted on my door along with other slurs...." Reed shrugged. "Those were just a few of the things I think he did."

"Why in the world would he call you a fag and those other things?"

"Makes it kind of hard to convince the local police that the ex was doing it when all they could see was a hate crime. I wasn't ashamed of being gay, but Peyton was." Reed pulled up to the window, paid, got the food, and pulled off. "The man isn't stupid, Taz. No, he's very smart actually. The police never looked at him. And I left town shortly after the last incident."

"Then it is imperative that we tell your family about him. He's a terrible person, and they should not be exposed to him. He's dangerous. Who knows what he might do?" Taz set his mouth in a determined line, as if everything was settled. Reed wished it was that easy.

"Look, babe." He sighed. "I can't do that. I can't drag them into the middle of my mess. It's not fair. He wouldn't hurt them. I know that's hard for you to understand or to believe, but it's just me, and once we leave here, things will go back to normal." Reed turned down the street his parents lived on, concentrating on the road. He was afraid if he looked at Taz, let him see into his eyes, he might see the truth—that Reed didn't want his family to know to what depths he had fallen with Peyton. What he'd permitted Peyton to do to him.

He couldn't stand knowing it himself, but to admit how he'd groveled, allowed Peyton to have control over him… that had to stay his own dirty little secret for the sake of his own sanity.

They'd arrived, and conversation was momentarily tabled by the business of bringing dinner inside and setting the table in the dining room. As he busied himself putting down plates and silverware, Reed wondered if Peyton had been here before, had shared meals with his parents in this very room. The thought sickened him. But what could he do about it? He wasn't one for confrontations. That's why he'd fled to New York. To get out from under Peyton's thumb, run away from the memories, and start a new life. And he had. Between his store and having Taz with him, everything was perfect and he was happier than he'd ever been.

So why was he so afraid that Peyton was going to fuck things up for him somehow? A tremor ran through his body, and a plate nearly slipped through his fingers. He was only dimly aware of Taz suddenly beside him. Taz slipped an arm around him and pulled him into the living room. They hadn't turned on the lights yet, but the shadows of evening were slipping inside, creating pockets of darkness. Before he quite realized what was happening, he found himself lying on the sofa beneath the front window that overlooked the street, his head cradled in Taz's lap.

Taz admitted to himself that he didn't understand Reed's fears, but he felt them, knew they existed. And, against his better judgment, he reluctantly agreed not to do or say anything to upset him any further. He loved Reed too much to do that. He just hoped Reed was right in this matter. He gently caressed Reed's cheek, willing him to relax.

"I will never let anyone hurt you," he whispered, his eyes intent on Reed's face, watching for any and every sign of his state of being. He was gratified to see some of the anxiety lessen as Reed melted into the couch and Taz's touch. He would do anything for Reed, even if it wasn't easy. Like not telling his family about the evil in their midst.

Their idyllic moment was interrupted as lights flashed inside the room, bounced off the wall and went out. "That must be them,"

Reed murmured, struggling to sit up. "Guess we should turn on the lights in here so they can see to come in."

Taz watched him rise, following him with reluctance. Reed had just turned on a floor lamp, and then the hurricane lamps that graced the tables on either side of the sofa, when the front door opened.

"Goodness, I was wondering why it was dark in here," Jeanette exclaimed. "I saw your car, so I figured you were here."

"Yeah, we're here, Mom. How's Dad?"

"Sleeping, when we left. Said he didn't want to see us again until tomorrow." She laughed. "Just like him to try to arrange everything, even from a sick bed. I'm hoping the doctor will tell us tomorrow when we can bring him home."

"That would be nice," Reed agreed. "Where's Renee?"

As if on cue, his sister stepped through the door, arm in arm with Peyton Wheeler. They were both laughing, and Reed's heart tightened at the sight. "Do I smell chicken?" Renee closed the door behind them, sniffing the air appreciatively. "Reed, you're a miracle worker! How'd you cook fried chicken so fast?" she teased.

"Very funny. It's takeout and you know it. I thought it would be easier all the way around. We can eat better when Dad gets home."

She ruffled his hair. "I love their fried chicken, bro, just giving you shit. Need some help with that?" Not waiting for an answer, she latched onto his arm and dragged him into the kitchen.

"Be right back. Make yourself at home, boys." Jeanette gave Taz and Peyton a warm smile before heading down the hall. Taz found himself alone with Peyton. He stared at him in silence, studying the other man carefully.

"So, you and Reed, huh?" Peyton began in a forced conversational tone. "How long have you been dating?"

"We're not dating. We live together."

Peyton's eyebrows shot straight up. "That's a bit fast, isn't it?" He took a step toward Taz, lowering his voice. "Since when has Reed been willing to commit to one guy?"

Taz met the other man's forceful gaze without flinching. "Since me," he said. "And I am not you." Leaving the words hanging in the air between them, he turned on his heel and walked out to the kitchen, afraid if he stayed another moment, he'd have to put his fist into Peyton's nose, and he knew that would upset Reed too much, so he could not do that.

REED IMMEDIATELY saw the change in his lover when Taz entered the room. Tension crackled around him, and he looked... well, damn. He looked like he wanted to rip someone apart. Reed had little doubt who'd caused this reaction, but still it was a shock to see this side of Taz. Maybe it was wrong of him, but he tended to think of his lover as being a little innocent, a little... playful, and fun-loving. There was nothing easygoing or fun-loving about him now. Oh no. His eyes were narrowed, his lips pinched tight, and frown lines creased the area between his eyes.

This was totally not the Taz he knew.

Seeing that his mom and sister were busy setting the table, he stepped closer to Taz. "Hey, babe, what's going on?" Reed kept his voice low so they wouldn't draw attention.

"I do *not* like your past boyfriend, Reed. He's not a pleasant person. I would like to put my fist into his nose, but I know that would upset you." Taz shrugged as the aforementioned person entered the room. "I don't see how your mom and sister can be so friendly with him."

"They don't know, remember? To them, he's nothing more than a family friend. But yeah, I know what you mean." Reed hugged Taz quickly, then walked him to the table. He did know what Taz meant. The fact that Peyton was hanging around his family made his skin crawl, but there was nothing he could say, not if he didn't want all the ugly facts to come out. While he doubted Peyton wanted his family to know about them any more than he did, it still made him uncomfortable. He was willing to bet his reasons for keeping everything under wraps were different than Peyton's. Reed heard a door shut and a voice drift down the hall. Oh lovely, the day just went to hell in a handbasket. Jacob had arrived.

"Hello? Mom? Where you at?"

"Back here, Jacob."

"Is that fried chicken I smell?" Jacob walked in, looked around, and scowled at Reed. "That smells really…. Oh, you're here. I had hoped…. Hey! Peyton! I didn't know you'd be here."

Reed's stomach dropped as he watched the two men shake hands like they were great friends or something. As he listened to them talk about getting together to play a round of golf, he wanted to scream. What the hell was Peyton doing? Didn't he know how Jacob felt about gay people? Jesus, Jacob would have a fit if he ever figured out Peyton had been in a relationship with his own brother. But, knowing Jacob, he'd just blame him… somehow. Probably think he'd turned Peyton gay or some nonsense. God, he wanted this day to just end. He wanted to hide away with Taz and forget all of it.

"You okay?" Taz asked.

"Been better. Let's just get this over with, then we can get out of here. Maybe go for a drive or hide out in our room. Something."

"Well, everyone have a seat and I'll say grace." Jeanette motioned to the table while Jacob glared at Reed again, but a sharp look from their mother cut off whatever Jacob had been tempted to say. This time.

THIRTY MINUTES later, Reed pulled Taz out of the house behind him. Dinner sat like a lead balloon in his stomach. That had to be one of the more unpleasant meals he'd had lately, but at least it was over. Jacob had kept his insults vaguely subtle, and Peyton had kept his mouth shut.

"Thank God that's over." Reed leaned against the railing that ran around the patio, his arms wrapped securely around Taz. Twilight covered the land, and the night creatures were waking up to greet the oncoming darkness. Crickets chirped and frogs croaked.

Turning slightly, Reed stared out over the lake, slowly relaxing. He loved to be near water, but the rivers that riddled New York City weren't exactly what he had in mind.

"Sorry that was so awful for you." Taz leaned his head back against Reed's shoulder. "At least Renee seems to like us. And your mom and dad."

"Ignore Jacob and Peyton, that's my best advice. In a few more days we'll be out of here and never have to see them again."

"Works for me."

"And you work for me." Reed tilted Taz's face toward his and kissed him softly. Taz reacted, pressing their lips together again when Reed released him, a small moan issuing from the back of his throat. Their bodies automatically drew closer, as if magnetized.

Taz placed one hand behind Reed's head, anchoring himself in his touch, willing him to forget all about his unpleasant sibling. Thank the gods Cal wasn't such an asshole. His older brother might have his ways, and a tendency toward order and organization, but he accepted Taz as he was.

He heard the sound of a door opening and closing, the clatter of footsteps on the deck; someone was coming out of the house, but his eyes were closed and he wasn't inclined to look to see who it was. Time enough for that. He was comfortable as he was. All too soon, though, he became aware of the identity of that person by his angry bellow.

"Don't you two have any shame? What if Mom or Renee saw you? Or the neighbors? Can't you at least show some decency and be queer in private?"

Taz felt Reed stiffen in his arms. Even in the dimmer light of evening, he could see the flush that overtook his lover's cheeks, feel the conflict that raged through his body. "Reed, don't let him get to you," he whispered. "He's not worth it."

"There's a special place for people like you," Jacob snarled. "They call it Hell. God puts all the homos there, and the liars and the murderers too." He took a step toward them, and Reed took a step away from both Taz and Jacob.

Taz stepped in between the two men, drawing himself to his full height. A low growl had replaced the moan, and it was directed straight at Jacob Hatcher. Taz felt his muscles tense, and the hair all over his body stand on end, his nails lengthening.

"Taz...." He heard Reed's voice, cautioning him, but he was too far gone to listen for the moment. Every protective instinct he had was in force. He wasn't about to let Jacob come between him and Reed if it took the last breath in his body to do it. Jacob might be bulkier than Taz, but Taz was fairly confident he could take him on if it came to that. He was stronger than he looked, and his survival instincts were high.

"Come on, Taz, let's just go inside." Reed stepped around Taz with every intention of dragging his lover back in the house if he had to. The last thing he wanted was a brawl on his parents' back patio. Although, to be honest, it wouldn't be the first time Jacob had swung at him, but they'd been kids then. Some things didn't change.

"Yeah, why don't you take your faggotty self back inside where decent folks don't have to look at stuff like that? Better yet, why don't you just go back to New York? I'm sure your kind fits in better there."

Reed saw red... literally. Of all the things to call him, that one word made his head explode and his temper spike. He spun around, unable to keep from responding to his brother's intentional slur. "You're such a goddamn idiot, Jacob. And it must really gripe your ass that I went to New York and made something of myself. Unlike you."

Jacob snarled. "How dare you use the Lord's name in vain? Blasphemer!"

"Tell you what? Why don't you stick the god you worship up your ass, hit the spin button, and rim yourself real good? You need something to loosen you up and a good ass fucking might do the trick. And I'll tell you something else... the God I worship loves us all. Besides—"

That was as far as Reed got. One second, Jacob was foaming at the mouth, and the next his fist was flying toward Reed's face. Before Reed could even react, however, another hand shot out and wrapped around Jacob's fist... the same fist that was on a crash course with Reed's jaw.

"I don't *think* so," Taz hissed.

All three men stood frozen: Jacob struggling against the strength that held him hostage, Taz furious that anyone would strike his lover, Reed with his mouth hanging open.

"Damn," Reed mumbled, goggling at Taz as Jacob strove to break Taz's hold. Reed knew firsthand how much power Jacob had in those bulky arms of his from other times they'd had occasion to fight. Taz must be strong... damn strong. Holy cow, he'd had no idea. His kitten just turned into a tiger right in front of his eyes. And, speaking of which, Taz really was starting to show some of his more... interesting traits. Not a good thing. "Babe." Reed put his hand over Taz's, the one that was wrapped around Jacob's fist. "This isn't the way. And I really need you to calm down, kitten." Reed hoped the use of Taz's nickname would catch his attention and get his point across. Now was *not* the time to go alien.

Even if he would enjoy watching Taz throw Jacob across the backyard. And something told him Taz could do it.

Taz didn't look at Reed, but a calmness seemed to come over him. Still holding Jacob's fist, he walked the nasty man back several steps, making his point—he was the stronger of the two.

"No one, and I mean *no one*, tries to hurt my Reed. This I won't allow. Consider this the only warning you get." Taz flung Jacob's fist away from him. "The *only* warning."

Jacob, panting, glared at Reed, but didn't say another word. Turning on his heel, he stalked back to the house, his pride hanging in tatters. The slamming of the back door snapped Reed out of his daze.

"Well, damn, babe. Just... damn." Reed ran a hand through his hair. "Got to say this is a side of you I've never seen before and I'm... damn impressed. Holy hell, am I impressed."

Taz curled himself into Reed, his anger at Jacob having been released, returning to kitten mode now that the immediate threat had been removed. "I will *never* let anyone bring harm to you, my Reed. Even if he is your brother."

Reed shot a quick glance into the night sky, and thanked again whatever lucky star had sent Taz in his direction. His guardian angel had certainly been looking out for him that night. Now, if only his angel could make sure that Reed's happiness wasn't fleeting, as had been his experience up until now. He was almost afraid to hope anymore.

SEVEN

REED AWOKE the next morning with a firm resolution. He wasn't going to just stand by and watch Peyton Wheeler weasel his way into his family. It was one thing when it was him and Peyton. Bad enough he'd let his ex get away with the things he had and kept quiet about them. Maybe if he'd spoken up then, his family wouldn't be in the danger they were in. Although just what that danger was, he wasn't sure. He just knew his ex was bad news. And if he hadn't been such a coward about admitting not only to their past relationship, but to Peyton's abuse... well, he knew there was no way that Mom or Dad, and certainly not Renee, would have ever brought the viper to their collective bosoms. Jacob was another matter entirely. He might have, just out of spite.

The question was could he actually tell them the truth after all these years? Not such an easy question to answer. But Reed knew he had to at least try. He'd never forgive himself if something happened to them because of him. Still, he had to do it the right way, take it slowly and ease into it. Yeah, it wasn't going to be nearly as easy as it seemed, even in theory.

He let Taz go into the shower first, resisting his pleas to come with him. Not that Reed wouldn't have loved to do just that, but in his parents' house? That didn't feel right. Coming home, even at his age, was a mindset thing, and it felt too awkward to even think about being naked with Taz with his mother and sister in the house. It also served a double purpose, though, in that he could open a dialogue with his mother without fear of Taz saying too much too soon. He knew if he told Taz not to say anything, he wouldn't understand. Taz was an open book, and he didn't understand anything less than total honesty.

Reed sighed. How he envied his lover that. How he wished he had the nerve to *be* like that. Maybe today would be the start of a new level of honesty.

He found his mother in the kitchen, making waffles and frying bacon.

"Morning, Mom!" He came up behind her and kissed the cheek she offered. "You didn't have to go to all that trouble for us."

"Speak for yourself, little bro."

To his dismay, Renee came plowing out of her bedroom, tugging a T-shirt into place over a pair of rather tight blue jeans. Momentarily distracted by the sight of his sister, he raised skeptical eyebrows.

"Do you use a can opener to get out of those things?"

"No, smartass, I don't." She stuck out her tongue. At the same moment, their mother admonished, "Language!"

Reed smirked, but the look slid off his face. "Ah, listen, guys, I wanted—"

Renee shoved a cup of coffee in Reed's hand. "Hey! Where's your better half?"

Reed frowned at Renee, the coffee nearly sloshing over the edge of the cup. "He's in the shower. Anyway—"

"Breakfast isn't ready yet, why don't we drink our coffee out on the back patio? It's a nice morning." Renee stared a hole through Reed.

Reed ran a hand through his hair. "But—"

"Oh heavenly day, go on with you." Jeanette stood at the stove, waving the spatula. "Your sister apparently wants to talk to you about something without me around. I promise I won't beat Taz over the head with a rolling pin or anything, sweetie, so go."

Renee grabbed Reed by the arm and marched him outside. No sooner had the door shut than Renee rounded on Reed. "Dammit, Reed."

"Dammit, *Reed*?" Reed sputtered. "Dammit, *Renee* is more like it. You're about as subtle as a bulldog in a cage fight. Jesus Christ, I was trying to talk to the two—"

"You do not need to tell Mom about what happened with you and Jacob last night. She doesn't need the extra stress, not on top of everything else she's dealing with." Renee leaned back against the railing, sipping her coffee. "I know what happened, and Mom would freak if she knew Jacob tried to hit you."

"I… that wasn't… but how did you…. Dammit, Renee. What were you doing, peeking out the window again? Thought you grew out of that by now. I got enough of that when we were kids."

Renee glared at Reed as a blush climbed up her cheeks. "I just happened to glance out the window, thank you very much, and I saw what happened. I was *not* spying." Suddenly Renee grinned and winked at Reed. "And speaking of the cutie—go, Taz! He certainly shut Jacob down from what I saw."

Reed blew on the hot coffee. "That was really out of character for him, but yeah, it made me feel good. God, did you see the look on Jacob's face? I'd pay good money to have a picture of that."

"Yeah, me too. I thought about taking one, but Mom would've wanted to know what was going on if I suddenly whipped out my cell. And if she had any idea how out of bounds Jacob was last night, I don't know what she'd have done. I do know she doesn't need that kind of shit right now, though."

"I totally agree, but I didn't start it, and damned if I'm going to let Jacob lay me out either. The bastard hasn't changed at all."

"Did you really expect him to? And unfortunately, he's not a bastard, as we both know. Bottom-feeder, yeah, but he *is* related to us, I'm afraid, by good old-fashioned blood. Unless maybe he was dropped off here by aliens and our parents hid the fact? Now *that* I could see. Some slimy, googly-eyed, brain-eating alien from outer space."

Reed strangled on his coffee, uncomfortable with the too-close-to-home turn the conversation had just taken. Speaking of aliens—there was Taz now, standing in the kitchen, talking to their mom, and he was as far away from a slimy brain-eating alien as one could get. "You need to watch something besides those sci-fi channels, girl. I mean, really. They're taking over your brain."

Renee giggled.

"Look, Taz is out of the shower. How about we go back inside? I promise I won't say anything to Mom." Relieved that she agreed without an argument or any further discussion of the Jacob is an alien theory, Reed followed Renee back into the kitchen. Guess that solved the problem of telling them about Peyton, effectively shelving the situation for now. Renee was right; his Mom didn't need any more stress.

Would there ever come a time when he could tell his family the truth about Taz? Reed had no frigging clue.

BREAKFAST WAS not only delicious, but it was blessedly peaceful, thanks in large part to Jacob's absence. His name did not even come up once, for which Reed was grateful. Even better, Taz outdid himself in being charming, which was saying a lot considering his lover fairly oozed charm from every pore. And not once did he say or do anything even remotely strange. Reed glowed every time he looked at him. He held his hand openly over the breakfast table and basked in the ability to be open and honest about who he was, for a change.

They split into two groups to travel to the hospital. Renee drove their mom, and Reed and Taz went together, but they would bring Reed's mom back as Renee had to go to the bar later and work for a while. Dad had called before they left, saying the doctor was optimistic that he could be discharged the next day so it was important that he talk to the family when they visited. Things were certainly looking up. If it continued in this way, he and Taz would be heading back home soon.

Home. The thought made him tingle. Home with Taz was a very special place, and while he loved his family, it would be good to be in their own space together again.

On the way to the hospital, he called Peter and put him on speakerphone so he wouldn't have to hold the cell while he drove.

"A Touch of Class, this is Peter, how may I help you?" The familiar voice answered the shop phone.

"Hey Peter, it's me!"

"Reed! How are things going? How's your dad?" Peter sounded unflappable as ever. Reed breathed an internal sigh of relief. If things were not going well, he was sure he would have heard it in Peter's voice.

"Dad's actually doing well. In fact, we're on the way there now. There's a chance he might be discharged tomorrow."

"That's really good, Reed. I'm glad. Will you be coming home then?"

"Not right away. I want to make sure he's doing okay, that he and my mom can handle everything, you know?"

"I know what you mean, Reed. That's cool."

"How's business?"

"Pretty good. Nothing earthshaking but a little better than normal for this time of year. I've taken care of the deliveries, ordered the things you asked me to. Everything's straight. Well, in a manner of speaking." He snickered at his own joke.

Reed laughed. "I can imagine. I'll let you know when I have some idea about coming back. I really appreciate your doing this for me. I owe you some time off for sure."

"I'll hold you to that." Peter chuckled. "Not that I have anywhere to go. Or anyone to go with."

Reed winced at his friend's words. He felt bad for Peter. He knew the shop had become his whole life. Peter's relationships with men never seemed to end well and, more often than not, he was left alone. But it wasn't like Reed was an expert on such matters himself. Taz had dropped into his lap—literally. Otherwise, he'd be in pretty much that same silly boat, searching for a paddle and a clue. He didn't have suitable gay friends to fix Peter up with, and he didn't allow dating in the customer pool. On the other hand, Peter's lack of a love life was fortuitous for occasions such as this.

"Yeah, well, you just never know when things will turn around for you. I'll check back when I know more. Call me if you need me, okay?"

Peter snorted. "Right. I'm fine, the shop is fine, just concentrate on your dad. Bye."

"Talk to you later." Reed hung up, the sigh he'd been holding in finally escaping.

"Is everything not okay?"

"Hmm? Oh yeah, babe, everything's fine at home. I was just thinking about Peter and his lack of a love life. I wish there was someone I knew who was gay and single." Reed maneuvered through the Florida traffic. To him, this was nothing; these people should try driving in New York. No wonder he didn't own a car there. He muttered when someone cut him off, thought about laying on the horn but decided against it.

"You don't know anyone?"

"I'm afraid not. I just don't have that many friends." Reed shrugged. Fact was he'd spent every spare second since arriving in New York in getting his business up and running. That hadn't left a whole lot of time for socializing. "We'll have to see what we can do once we get home. I owe Peter some time off. Maybe he'll actually go on vacation, but I doubt it. Not much fun going somewhere by yourself."

"I know that is very true." Taz patted Reed's hand. "We'll figure out something."

Reed felt reassured just by hearing Taz say *we*. A simple word, but it meant so much, told him that they were both in it for the long haul, and that was a mighty good feeling to have.

Reed pulled into one of the hospital parking lots, paid the toll, and turned the car off. There was something else besides his employee's love life he needed to talk to Taz about before they walked inside. Best get it over with now.

"Look, Jacob is probably here, so let's try not to upset Dad by ripping out my brother's guts or something. Even though we may want to. Okay, Taz?" Reed leaned across the seat and kissed his lover. "I want you to know I found you defending me the sexiest thing ever, but don't take any chances, love. Just ignore him, please?"

"He annoys me, almost as much as that other one." Taz growled.

"See? That's what I'm talking about. Humans don't growl." Reed waited until Taz opened the door, then popped the master lock on the driver's side. "Even though I find that sound very… arousing."

Taz hiked an eyebrow. "You do?" He gave a faux growl for good measure, then turned serious once more. "Okay, I'll keep that in mind. They just…. I'll try, Reed. I don't want to do anything that would set your dad's recovery back or bring trouble down on us. So, as much as I'd like to flex my claws, I won't."

"Good." Reed grabbed Taz's hand as they entered the hospital. "Hopefully, we'll be leaving soon and things can get back to normal. For all of us."

They rode up to Herb's floor holding hands since they were alone in the elevator, dropping them as they exited the car. Reed nodded at the nurses as they passed by the nursing station. Just as his hand landed on the door, he heard Jacob's voice float out. Taking a deep breath, he reminded himself of the lecture he'd just given Taz, his desire to punch Jacob in the nose nearly overwhelming him. Then Peyton's voice joined the mix, and he found himself taking another deep breath. For just a moment, he imagined himself as a young Jackie Chan, whirling into their midst, karate chopping his enemies into oblivion; they'd never know what hit them. Then he and Taz could ride off into the sunset… Taz's voice drew him out of his reverie.

"Well, at least we know they're here," Taz said.

"Yippee ki-yay." Reed pushed the door open. The good news was the doctor was there already. At least they wouldn't have to be alone with the Hardy boys.

An older man, thin on top with graying hair that grew thickly about his ears, and a short gray stubble on his chin, he had warm brown eyes that somehow inspired confidence at first glance. He stood at the end of the bed, eyeing them as they walked in.

"More visitors, Herb? Looks like you're popular today."

"Those two are our other boys." Reed's father shifted in the bed, using the bed tray that lay over his lap to pull himself into a sitting position. His wife, who stood beside him, reached down to assist him. "The one with the short hair's Reed. The long hair belongs to Taz. Boys, meet the best doctor in all of Lake Hydethorne, Dr. Winters."

"Glad to meet you." Reed held out his hand and the physician took it; his grip was firm, instilling more trust. "How's Dad doing?"

Dr. Winters released Reed's hand, took Taz's, and smiled at them both. "Your dad's doing great. In fact, I was just about to give him the good news. You're just in time."

Reed glanced around the already crowded room. His sister was standing far too close to Peyton for his liking, although he knew she was perfectly safe from any unwelcome overtures on his part, even if she didn't realize it. Jacob sat on the opposite side of the bed; he'd scooted his single chair so far over at their entrance, he was almost in the next bed. Good thing it was unoccupied. His parents were together, as always. Without analyzing his own motives, Reed stepped closer to Taz, surreptitiously reaching for his hand.

"Well, what is it?" Herb asked the question that was on everyone's minds.

"I'm afraid I'm kicking you out tomorrow," Dr. Winters said, maintaining a straight face.

"Can't think of any other tests you might want to charge me for?" Reed's father chuckled even as he spoke.

"No, I ran out, so out you go. Jeanette, you can come for him in the morning. Anything after about nine, let's say. Does that work for you?"

"You know it." She beamed at her husband, and then at each of her children.

Dr. Winters covered all the do's and don'ts, pointed his finger at Herb a few times when the patient groaned, reminded him that all instructions would be included with his discharge papers, and left.

"Well, Dad, seems like you've overstayed your welcome here." Reed smiled as he moved closer to the bed. "And stop frowning so much. You knew a change was coming."

"He's frowning because he's trying to figure out how he's still going to get that bowl of ice cream before bedtime." Jeanette shook her head fondly at her husband. "Which he's not."

"Don't see the difference one damn bowl will make," Herb griped, straightening the covers.

"Dad," Renee whined, rolling her eyes. "Do you *want* to be back in here?"

"Well, this did get Reed to come home."

Jacob snorted, and Reed fought off the cringe that threatened to overtake him. "Oh man, come on, Dad. That's not funny. You scared the crap out of me... out of all of us. Besides, I told you—"

"I know, son. I was just kidding. I'll do what the doctor said." Herb leaned his head back on the pillows and let out a deep breath. "This scared me too. Just about the time your mother and I were getting ready to get on with the golden years, this smacks us in the face. We got plans, and this certainly put things in perspective."

"Yes, you never know what will happen in your life to put things into a proper perspective," Peyton agreed. "A good scare will open your eyes to a great many things."

Reed wanted to tell Peyton to shut the hell up. He didn't know exactly what Peyton meant, but the brief stare he got while his ex reeled out his words of wisdom made him uncomfortable. Frankly, he didn't give a damn what enlightenment Peyton had stumbled upon, he just wanted the ass to go away.

"So, we should be here kind of early in the morning, huh?" Renee said. "That'll give us time to clean all the goodies out of the kitchen tonight."

"You are a mean, mean daughter," Herb grumbled.

"And too late anyhow," Jeanette added. "Already done it."

Conversation flowed for another hour. Reed stood and fished around in his pockets. "Going to get something to drink. I'll be back in a minute."

"Want me to help?" Taz looked up from the web picture of different hair colors Renee had on her smart phone.

"That's okay, babe, I'll just be a minute. I'd hate to interrupt that fascinating conversation about hair dyes the two of you have going on."

Renee snorted. "I'm going to figure out how to get all those different colors like he has in my hair if it's the last thing I do."

"Yeah, good luck with matching Taz's hair color, you're gonna need it." Reed winked at Taz as he walked out of the room. Little did his sister know just how much luck she was going to need.

Laughing to himself, he walked down to the little room that housed the snack and soda machines, wondering what sort of selection he might find, trusting that there must be a high turnover rate so everything would be fresh. But a dismal sight met his eyes.

"Out of service? Really?" Reed glared at the sign that proclaimed the machines didn't work. "Just great."

A nurse walked by and suggested he try the snack area on the floor below them. With a quick nod of thanks, he headed for the elevators. He really didn't want to leave Taz by himself for too long, not with Peyton and Jacob. The potential for disaster was just too great. One of them would have been bad enough, but two was asking for trouble. Just as the elevator doors were about to close, a hand shot through the opening. The door stopped in its track, and slid open again.

"Thought I'd get something too," Peyton said.

Holy shit, kill me now.

Reed automatically retreated to a corner of the car as his ex advanced inside. There wasn't very far he could go, but he glared at Peyton, hoping *that*, and a bit of common sense, would keep Peyton on his own side. No such luck. As the doors shut with a clang and the elevator lurched down to the next floor, Peyton stepped closer to Reed.

Reed tried to move away, but he was already at the wall and had nowhere else to go. Damn.

"I'm glad Herb's doing so well," Peyton began. He ran his hand through his dark hair, accidentally brushing it against Reed's arm in the process. Reed flinched.

"Yeah, me too," he mumbled. He cast a wary glance at his ex.

"Guess you'll be heading back to the Big Apple soon, huh?"

"What we do is none of your business," Reed replied pointedly. For some reason, Peyton's grin only grew wider. Like he was in the middle of some big private joke, one which Reed was afraid he was the punch line for.

The elevator jarred to a stop, and Reed rushed through the doors once they were wide enough to allow him to do so. He began to walk down the hall, eyeing the doors he passed, looking for any sign of artificial nutrition to be had. To his dismay, Peyton kept pace with him.

"No offense meant, Reed. I'm just concerned about Herb, that's all. I figured now that the crisis is over, you'd be wanting to get back to what's important."

There. He saw them. Gleaming rows of silver handles, waiting to be turned, dispensing assorted snacks, while in the second tier, a can of heaven awaited the punch of a button. He bit back his first response, not wanting Peyton to know how close to home his words hit. He was also suddenly grateful Taz hadn't accompanied him. He suspected his kitten would not take any of this lying down. Best he stay out of the ugliness.

"I don't need to answer to you." Damn, his answer was an answer anyway. He stared into the vending machine that held the soft drinks and selected one that carried a pretty good punch, aimed his quarters into the slot and let them drop. When the light told him the machine was ready, he jabbed at the buttons with his thumb and down it dropped.

He could hear Peyton make his selection from the machine beside him, and looked up to see him holding a candy bar aloft. "I remember how much you always liked these," he said softly.

"You'd tell me that sometimes you just felt like a nut. And then I'd say that I always felt like having nuts. As long as they were yours." He grinned at his own words, and Reed's cheeks heated.

Damn, Peyton had a way of making him feel dumb. And unclean.

"Yeah, well, enjoy." He tried to exit the too-small room, but Peyton seemed to be taking up more space than the law should allow and he couldn't get by without touching him, something he was quite loath to do.

"I miss you, Reed." Peyton had dropped his voice into a seductive whisper, one that raised the hackles on Reed's neck, but not in a good way.

"Don't, Peyton. Just back it up. We tried having a relationship and it didn't work, remember? I've moved on, and I'm very happy with Taz. You need to do the same. With someone else," he hastily added, just in case his ex got any funny notions of going after his man. He wouldn't put it past him. Reed skirted around Peyton, intent on evading whatever the other man might be thinking of doing. "And while it's on my mind, I have no idea what you think hanging out with my family's going to accomplish, but you should know if Jacob ever found out we used to be together, he'd drop you like a hot potato. He's not overly fond of gays. Or hadn't you noticed?"

"I'm not worried about your brother." Peyton reached out to Reed, his hand catching air as Reed moved back. "And as far as that boy you're seeing… please. He can't give you what I can."

"Right. What you gave me was an inferiority complex that took me a good long while to get over. Pardon me if I'm not all that interested in repeating that. Just leave me alone, Peyton."

Reed turned and hurried down the hall. He stabbed at the elevator button, mind made up—if Peyton tried to get back on with him, he'd bail out, take the damn stairs if he had to. Once the doors closed, he leaned shakily against the back wall and took a deep breath. No Peyton. Now all he had to do was calm down before he got back to his dad's room, otherwise Taz would know immediately there was something wrong with him. His gut instinct told him that wouldn't be a good thing.

EIGHT

TAZ TRIED not to pace the floor of the hospital room, but with all the energy inside of him that demanded to be released, it was a near thing. The best he could manage was to tap his foot, although that wasn't all that satisfactory. And it earned him more than one dirty look from Reed's brother. Which was no kind of deterrent from Taz's point of view, but he had to stay mindful of Reed's parents and sister and try to behave himself.

When Peyton got up to leave just after Reed did, Taz nearly followed him from the room. He knew, just knew, Peyton was going to talk to Reed, and it made him mad.

What was this guy's problem? The only reason he didn't follow him was because Renee was going on and on about hair color and wanting to know about his, and he couldn't figure out a way to just get up and leave, not without being rude to his Reed's sister, and that he refused to do.

The door to the hospital room opened and Reed walked in. At last. Taz anxiously searched his face…. He might appear fine to someone else, but Taz knew his lover well enough to know that he really wasn't. His lips were pressed into a tight line, and his face was too pale. All bad signs. Reed crossed the room and stood next to him, uncharacteristically silent. Taz could feel the repressed anger rolling off Reed, but there was something else too.

Taz looked up at Reed. He wanted to say something, but he didn't dare. He realized he needed to save his words for a more private moment. Instead, he squeezed Reed's hand, his very cold hand. Reed looked down at him, and his facial features relaxed somewhat. Reed took a deep breath, closed his eyes for a moment, then opened them. A small nod and a mouthed "later" told Taz all he needed to know. Taz vaguely listened as everyone around them talked, but his attention and his eyes were on Reed. Until the point at which Peyton entered the room a little while later and Reed stiffened up again. Taz decided he'd had enough.

"Reed? I'm getting hungry. How about you and I go find something to eat?"

Jeanette spoke up quickly. "You boys go on ahead. I think we'll probably do the same. It is getting on to lunchtime, isn't it? Then I need to go home and clean house before your father comes home tomorrow."

"And I need to check on the bar, actually," Renee spoke up, even as Herb began to protest.

"You don't need to do that, dear. Go home and get some rest. You'll wear yourself out. I don't need you waiting on me, Jeanette."

"Mom, you know we'll help," Reed added, before replying to Taz. "Good idea, babe. Hang on a sec."

Taz felt a rising tension in the room that he couldn't identify, one that was trying to settle in his chest. He simply wanted to get Reed away... from Jacob, from Peyton... from anything bad that might harm him. He wanted to be alone with Reed, make the rest of the world go away.

Taz tried not to fidget too much as everyone talked at once, their words tumbling over one another to the point of being chaotic. Finally Jeanette put her foot down and everything was settled, pretty much to everyone's satisfaction. Herb persuaded his wife that the house was just fine, that she was a wonderful housekeeper, and that she should just remember to pick him up the next day but please go home now. Renee had persuaded her mother to come to the bar to get a bite. She included Jacob too, but the tardy invitation was almost an afterthought, one that he haughtily rejected without a second's hesitation, to Renee's obvious relief—which she didn't bother to hide.

Reed moved to his father's bedside, trying not to step on his sister's feet, but it was close quarters on that side of the room and hard to maneuver. She gave him a cheeky look. "You're cooking dinner tomorrow, remember? And none of that fast food sh—stuff, either," she hastily amended.

"I know, I know." Reed bent down and kissed his father's cheek. "See you tomorrow, Dad. We'll come pick you up. What time should we be here?"

"I can do that," Jacob protested. "Don't worry about it. Take your fag—" An angry glare from Herb choked his words off midsentence. His mouth tautened into a grim line as he turned away, but even in profile, his anger was apparent.

"You can discuss that with your mother later." Herb turned back to Reed, reaching for his hand. "You two go on, I'll be fine. Worry about each other for a while."

"Thanks, Dad." Reed squeezed his father's hand then moved aside for Taz, who bent down and kissed Herb's cheek as well. When he straightened, he glared at Jacob who, if he even noticed, wisely made no comment.

Taz and Reed exchanged hugs with both Jeanette and Renee, while Jacob was conveniently ignored, although Taz noticed that seemed to suit Reed's brother just fine. Amid promises to see the women later, Taz and Reed finally exited the hospital room for the elevator. They had no chance to speak there as others crowded into the car after them, heading down toward the lobby as well, probably for similar reasons. It wasn't until they reached the parking lot once more that they were alone at last. Well, relatively speaking.

Taz stopped in the middle of the parking lot. Since his hand was tucked into Reed's, that forced the other man to stop too. He turned and looked back at Taz inquisitively. Taz didn't waste any time getting to the heart of the matter. "What did he say to you?"

Reed flushed and looked down, scuffing his shoe against the asphalt. "It doesn't matter," he said softly. "It's over and done with, and it won't happen again."

Taz reached up and tilted Reed's head back, looking into his eyes. "It does matter," he insisted. "You matter. Reed, you're everything to me. Please, don't have secrets from me."

Reed's face flushed. He sucked in his lower lip, biting at it. "I know, Taz, I do know. It's just that… I don't want him to ever be an issue between us. Not that he could be," he hastily added, watching Taz's temper rise. "Not like that. But if I repeat what he said, that only gives it value, and I don't want it to mean anything to you because it sure don't mean a thing to me. Do you know what I mean?"

"No." Taz shook his head. Reed sighed.

"If I were to tell you and you were to say something to him, then he'd know he got to us, and I don't want him to affect our lives in that way. He's not important to me, you are. I love you, Taz, and I only want to be with you, now and forever." He reached up and cupped Taz's cheek. "Sweet baby, you are everything to me. I love you more than I probably can ever express, but I'm sure going to try."

He drew Taz to him, their lips meeting. By the time they drew back, nothing more needed to be said, and they continued on to the car, arms about one another's waists, Taz's head on Reed's shoulder.

"What do you feel like eating?" Reed asked.

"I'm not sure, what would you like?"

"I wouldn't mind some barbecue," Reed admitted, glad that things were settled. "It's not as good as what I used to get in Mississippi, but it's a damn sight better than what you can—" He broke off in midsentence as they reached the rental car. There was something different about it, something that hadn't been there when they'd left. Namely, the single red rose that was held in place on the windshield by one of the wipers.

A chill ran up Reed's back as he stared at the flower. "What the fuck?"

Taz frowned at the car. "Huh. Why is there a flower on your car? Is that normal? Do your people do stuff like that at hospitals for some reason I'm unaware of? Like an offering to the gods of sickness?"

Reed thought he was going to be sick; the cramping in his gut left little doubt of that. Out of nowhere his head started pounding, and he had to remind himself not to squeeze Taz to bits. All he could see was that damned red rose. Oh God, what the hell was that thing doing on his car, and how had it gotten there?

"Reed? Is that something the hospital does to thank you for visiting—?" Taz reworded his question, as if to elicit a response. He turned to face his lover, his mouth falling open. "By the stars, are you okay?"

"I… no, that's not something the hospital does, Taz. I'm not sure why that's there." Reed swallowed, removing his arm from around Taz.

The lie lay on his tongue, foul and nasty. He hated red roses, hated them with a passion. The only time they'd ever showed up was when he and Peyton had particularly bad fights, the ones that ended with Peyton hurling insults like verbal javelins until Reed finally broke down and cried. Peyton always bought a red rose after every such incident, almost like a reward, when Reed capitulated and admitted he was silly or stupid. Like a flower could make up for the hate-filled words that often bounced around in Reed's head for weeks after.

There was only one person in the world who knew how Reed felt about red roses. He shivered at the thought.

Taz turned Reed away from the sight of the car. "You're pale. And you're shaking." Taz took Reed's face in his hands. "You may not know why that rose is there, but it's upsetting you. Why, Reed?"

"I, I… ah God, Taz. It's something Peyton used to do, back when we were…. He used to give me a red rose after we'd had an argument. He'd say the most hateful things, then later he'd try to make it all better by giving me gifts. A red rose was just one of the assorted things he'd bring home to try and fix us."

"That son of a whynore!" Taz growled, his hands fisting. "How dare he? Next time I see him, I'm going to—"

Reed shook his head. "Please don't, Taz. We don't *know* he did this, babe. Trust me, he'll never admit it if he's trying to play his damn mind games on me again. Best thing to do is ignore it."

"But he's *upsetting* you," Taz hissed.

"Easy there, kitten." Reed pulled Taz closer, holding that tight body near him as the feeling of sickness slowly retreated. Taz's love blanketed him, washing away the ugliness. "And that's how he gets his jollies. I let the damn thing throw me, and shame on me for doing that."

Taz wrapped his arms around Reed. "I want him to just leave us alone. You have enough stress right now without him adding to it. I don't understand why he's doing this."

Reed held tight for a minute, then stepped back. "He's the kind of person that doesn't like to lose, Taz. See, *I* broke up with him, then I moved clear across the country. If he'd done the breaking up, then I probably wouldn't even draw his attention because *he* would have been done first. I bruised his ego, babe, and a man like that doesn't handle rejection well. That's all this is about. If it's even him. We don't know he put that rose there. Anyone could have, and for any reason too. The car is sitting out in the open, after all. Not exactly hidden." He didn't really believe that, but if it kept Taz in check, then all the more reason to endorse that particular theory and at least throw out some doubt as to Peyton's guilt.

Taz glared at the rose. "But you think he did." It wasn't a question, but a statement. He wasn't fooling Taz one little bit. Reed sighed.

"Yeah, I do." Reed pulled the rose from the windshield wiper. With a glance at Taz, he dropped the rose on the ground and crushed it underfoot. *Boy, does that feel good.* With a grin, he opened the door for Taz. "And that's what I think about his stupid, juvenile stunt. Let's go eat, babe."

They got their barbecue platters to go in Styrofoam containers stacked inside of paper bags. They carried the food inside the house and ate it at the kitchen table. Despite having wanted it, Reed's appetite was poor, and he finally gave up any pretense that he was actually going to eat and set his food into the refrigerator for later.

Taz's heart ached for his lover. He wanted to do something—anything—to help, but he didn't know what. They cleaned up the kitchen, removing all trace of the meal, then went into the living room, taking seats next to one another on the couch.

Reed leaned over Taz and scooped up the remote from the far cushion. He turned on the television and began to surf, but nothing held his attention for more than two seconds. Finally, he gave up and clicked it off, tossing the remote where it had been in disgust. "Wish it was football season," he mumbled, leaning back into the cushions, closing his eyes.

"Hmmm, why's that?" Taz took advantage of this opportunity to gaze unabashedly at his lover, drinking in everything about him that he loved so much. He'd never seen someone so beautiful in his life as his Reed.

"'Cause then we could watch it, you know?"

"No, I don't know," Taz admitted.

"Oh yeah, I guess the Super Bowl was over before we met, wasn't it? Well, football is a sport. You know about sports, right? Well, this one involves two teams, and the object of the game is to score points. And, um, there's this ball... the football... it's made of pigskin—"

"It's made of what?" Taz inched closer to Reed, setting his hand over the knee closest to him, rubbing it gently.

Reed chuckled. "I know, right? But yeah, it's made of pigskin. Well, it was. I don't think so anymore. Anyway, both teams try to get the ball across the goal line to score a touchdown. That's the best way to score points, although kicking a field goal works too."

Taz didn't understand, but he let Reed keep talking; it seemed to make him happy and kept his mind off other things. "You mean they get points for kicking someone? Isn't that a little barbaric?"

"Oh no, babe, a field goal isn't a person. It's just what they call it when they kick the ball in between the goal posts. It's the name for that particular way to score, but it's only worth three points. A touchdown is worth seven. Well, six, plus the extra point. Sometimes they don't get the extra point, but usually they do...."

Taz wasn't really focused on the conversation. While Reed was talking, he'd been snaking his hand up along Reed's thigh, and he'd moved on to his groin. He cupped his crotch, producing a small moan. Gratified at the reception of his advances, Taz began to massage Reed's cloth-encased cock. He could feel it stir beneath the palm of his hand.

"Babe, what are you doing?"

"If you have to ask, I must be doing something wrong."

"Oh no, you're not, it's just...." He interrupted his own words with another groan. Taz had suddenly bent his head down between Reed's legs, his mouth lipping Reed's growing erection. "It's just...." He floundered and then gave up. "Oh God, Taz," he moaned.

Taz sucked at the fabric, drawing Reed's hardness with it. Reed squirmed beneath his touch. "Jesus, keep that up and I'll have an accident." He started to rise, but Taz took advantage of his change in position, pushing him back lengthwise onto the cushions. He removed his mouth long enough to unzip Reed's pants and slide his hand inside, wrapped his fingers around Reed's pulsing cock. With the other hand, he attempted to push Reed's trousers down, but it wasn't easy, and he was loath to relinquish his grasp of his lover.

"Help me, please?" he requested, and felt Reed lift his hips. Together they pushed the offending fabric down far enough that it was no longer a hindrance. Yet.

Taz slid his hand over the top of Reed's dick, picking up the slight wetness there, enough to ease the passage of his hand along the length as he began to pump it with purpose. He stole a glance at Reed. His head was thrown back, his eyes closed, his lips parted, a bit of pink tongue protruding, and his hands clutched at the couch as if to anchor himself to it. Still watching Reed, Taz slid onto the couch in between Reed's legs before he took him into his mouth in one gulp. He felt the tremendous shudder that overtook Reed. He arched into Taz's touch, stiffening.

"Damn...."

Taz began to suck, sliding up and down Reed's shaft, pouring all of the love he felt for this man into his movements. He maneuvered his hands into position, rolling Reed's balls, loving the feel of them against his flesh, loving the taste of him in his mouth.

"Babe, please... stop...."

Surprised, Taz paused, looking up at Reed. What had he done wrong? He panted slightly, and pulled off long enough to take a breath, his eyes turned inquisitively to his lover.

"No, no," Reed hastened to assure him. "Not that... but I need you... need to be in you.... Please... climb on top of me...."

That Taz could understand. "I want you in me, Reed, I do." He'd had hopes that they'd end up that way, but he certainly hadn't intended to push for it. However, since it was Reed's idea.... He leaned back and worked at the button to his own pants, unzipping it hastily, but he wasn't in the best position to be getting undressed, and he had to untangle their legs long enough to push them down. Then he realized he couldn't make do with only lowering them. He had to remove them. That involved taking off shoes and socks, so by then it only made sense to help Reed get naked too. At least from the waist down. But once he'd sorted it out, with Reed's frantic assistance, he bent down and kissed the tip of Reed's cock, which had started to abate in the interim, and licked it back to life before he moved into position and lowered himself slowly, very slowly, onto Reed.

"Oh God, you are so fucking tight. Go slowly, babe."

Taz, mouth partly open, slid down, inch by inch, the burn of penetration hitting him. The lack of lube slowed things down, but Taz was determined to have all of Reed inside him. He needed this. They both needed this. That asshole human had messed with Reed's confidence, and he wasn't having that. As his weight carried him down, he moaned as Reed's thick cock filled him, opening him wide. Reed's hands held his hips, and they both groaned from the feeling of heat and tightness.

"So good," Reed mumbled.

Taz leaned forward, his forehead resting against Reed's, his dick nestled against Reed's belly. "I love you, Reed. Every glorious bit of you…. You're perfect to me. *Never* think otherwise."

"Babe…." Reed sighed, the tilt of his lips saying plainly how much he needed to hear that.

"Now, I'm going to *make* love to you." Taz straightened and rested his hands on Reed's shoulders and wiggled slightly. Ah, no more burn, just that lovely feeling of fullness.

Taz pushed Reed's shirt up; he needed to touch as much of his man as possible. Carefully, he rose up, then eased down, his hands flexing on Reed's shoulders. Better, much better. Reed's head had fallen back against the couch, pleasure flushing his cheeks, his eyes closed. Which was good, but he wanted more. Using his legs, Taz moved up and down Reed's cock, speeding up as he bounced, his aching dick thumping against his stomach. Reed's eyes snapped open and Taz hissed with need as Reed's hands moved to his ass, holding both cheeks firmly.

"That's it, kitten. Fuck yourself on my dick."

Taz's hands scraped down Reed's chest, his claws out. Reed arched as pale lines appeared, showing proudly against Reed's chest. Those pretty little nipples of Reed's called to him and he grasped them both, twisting as he rode Reed.

"Mmm, babe, your stripes are showing," Reed panted.

"That's not all." Taz's grin was quick, a flash of joy that turned into a yelp of pleasure when Reed slammed him down hard. Taz's tail whipped about them, fluttering madly, while soft purrs filled the space around them.

Suddenly Reed held Taz still, holding him tightly so he couldn't move. Taz meowed pitifully, straining to be released.

"Hold on." Reed pulled Taz against his chest, his hands leaving Taz's ass.

"What—?" Taz let out a startled purr of happiness when Reed undid his braid, loosening his hair and spreading it out over his shoulders. Mollified, a grinning Taz shook his head, sending waves of multicolored hair everywhere.

Taz blinked when Reed reached up, his hand holding Taz's chin so they could look into each other's eyes. "You are so beautiful, Taz. Stripes, tail, all that sexy long hair…. You mean the world to me, my lovely little alien. You, and only you, complete me."

"Oh, Reed." Taz bit his lip to keep the tears back. "I feel the same."

When Reed released his chin, Taz closed the distance between them and kissed Reed, a gentle brush of lips, then giggled when Reed's hand slapped down on his ass. That was all the motivation he needed to get back to what he was doing… riding Reed for all he was worth.

"I'm going to fuck you so good, Reed. Going to make you yell when you come."

"Yeah?" Reed gasped as Taz slammed down. "Then ride me, babe. Spurt that load all over my chest."

Reed shifted his hips, and Taz yowled. That hard cock of Reed's was now nailing his hot spot every time. Reed might not be the only one yelling. He bounced in Reed's lap, driving both of them closer to the edge.

"Going… going to…." Taz threw his head back, purring frantically.

"Do it for me. Paint me, babe."

One more hard hit to his hot spot and Taz hissed long and loud as come spurted from his dick, covering Reed's chest. Before he could draw another breath, Reed thrust up hard and held his hips tightly, a strangled groan escaping from his lips. Warmth flooded Taz, filling him up as Reed came.

"Oh fuck," Reed groaned, holding Taz desperately as he unloaded.

Taz collapsed against Reed's chest, laughing softly. "Good gods, it just keeps getting better. I think we both needed that."

Reed ran his hands through Taz's hair. "I agree. And now we need to shower before we end up stuck together."

Taz nipped Reed's bottom lip and gently lifted himself off Reed. "Shower together?"

"Absolutely." Reed picked up the clothes thrown all over the place. "Head on in and get the water going. I'll get some clothes from our room."

"Don't be long!" Taz winked at Reed then hurried out of the room.

They made love again in the shower, and by the time they got out, they were wet but sated. They toweled one another off, donned clean clothes, and decided to be lazy. They ran out to a convenience mart and bought an assortment of taquitos, fresh from the grill. Taz had never seen such things before, and he was enchanted by the various flavor combinations. So of course they had to get two of everything. Along with tortilla chips, corn chips, and potato chips. And fountain drinks to wash it all down.

"That's a lot of food there, babe," Reed playfully observed.

Taz didn't take offense, and he found room for every single bite, licking his fingers most thoroughly when he was done.

"Here, that's my job." Reed laughed. They were ensconced on the sofa once more, a greasy paper trail spread across the coffee table before them. Reed took one of Taz's fingers and put it between his lips, sucking at it. Taz moaned.

"Oh damn, Reed, keep that up, and I might just have to give you a ride this time," he teased, although Reed read something else in his lover's eyes, something that said that if Reed said the word, he'd be more than ready and willing.

Reed took another finger into his mouth, sucking hard, his hand reaching for Taz, his fingers beginning to reach beneath his shirt. But the sound of the door put an end to that, and right quickly, as they hastily changed positions. Reed picked up a magazine, while Taz scattered the papers with one hand. They fell onto the floor.

"Babe, what—?"

No time to think or reply. He held the magazine to his face, as Taz spread himself out on the couch, his head nestled in Reed's lap, another periodical in his hands.

"Hello boys," Jeanette greeted them. Renee was right behind her. She carried a takeout bag from the bar in one hand. Her purse was gripped in the other.

"We didn't interrupt anything, did we? I mean, just carry on...." She gave them a wicked grin. Reed glanced down at Taz, who returned it without reservation.

"Renee, behave yourself. You're making your brother blush." Jeanette winked at them before taking the bag from Renee, heading out to the kitchen. Renee took up a position at the end of the couch, arms crossed, eyebrows raised.

"I know you two are not just sitting there reading like the sweet angels y'all are pretending to be."

"Oh? What makes you think not?" Reed asked with faux indignation.

"I'll tell you what makes me think not." Renee advanced toward them and jabbed her finger at Reed's magazine. "First off, that's upside down."

Reed's face flamed even higher. He'd paid so little attention to what was in his hands, he hadn't noticed.

"And secondly, that's Dad's issue of *Field & Stream* Taz has, and I just know he doesn't care about anything in that. Want me to dig out some of my old copies of *Playgirl*? I think I have some stashed in the attic."

"*Playgirl*?" Taz curiously asked. "What is that?"

"Naked men! Glorious naked men! Like *Playboy*, only with dicks. And the fiction pretty well sucks."

"Oh, okay, but I don't need to see pictures of naked men. I just saw Reed—"

Reed had tried to interrupt his speech—he'd had a bad feeling Taz was about to give something away—but no matter how much he tightened his grip on Taz's arm, he kept talking. And then it was too late.

Renee threw her head back and began to laugh. An embarrassed Reed extricated himself from Taz, and hastily began to pick up the scattered remains of their meal.

"I brought you guys back some appetizers, but I see you've eaten already. Or could you eat again?"

Reed balled the papers up in his hands, regaining some measure of control. He turned his gaze upon Taz, and found himself suffused with a warmth of a different sort. This scene… being here with his mom and his sister… and the man he loved more than anything. A great feeling of belonging, of rightness, overwhelmed him, a happiness he'd once thought could never be his. It took his breath away.

"You know what, I bet we could." He laughed, swiping at his eye, but trying to cover it up. "Want to watch a movie or something?"

"Sounds good to me."

"Me too." His mom entered the room, a cup of coffee in her hand. "I made a fresh pot, if anyone's interested."

When Taz started to stir, Reed hastily interjected. "I think we'll stick to water, thanks." Last thing he needed was an overly caffeinated kitten just before bedtime. "What did you want to watch?"

"I dunno." Renee shrugged. "What about you?"

Reed thought for a moment. Some things were not right to watch with family, and he didn't remember what they owned anymore.

"I'm in the mood for a classic," Jeanette announced. "Taz, do you like flying monkeys?"

"Flying monkeys?" Taz echoed, his eyes growing wide.

"You'll love these flying monkeys," Reed hastily interjected. He leaned down, putting his mouth against Taz's ear. "Not real ones, I promise."

"Oh, too bad. I would have liked to see that." He looked up at Reed's mom. "I would enjoy seeing your not-real flying monkeys," he said politely.

"You are just so precious." Jeanette smiled. She rummaged in the DVD cabinet, before pulling out a case. Renee brought the appetizers from the kitchen on plates that she laid on the coffee table. Reed threw the trash away and poured two large glasses of ice water. He and Taz settled together on one end of the couch, Renee taking the other. Jeanette took the recliner as they all settled in for an evening with the inhabitants of Oz. *A very peaceful evening indeed.*

NINE

SUNLIGHT FILTERED into the room, waking Reed. Stretching, he looked over at Taz who was curled close against him. Last evening had been thoroughly enjoyable. Jacob hadn't bothered to join them, which meant the atmosphere was easy and fun without his older brother's oppressive presence. There'd been no nasty remarks to deal with, no restraining his lover from punching Jacob's lights out, tempting though that idea was. And watching Taz's reaction to the movie had been entertaining. When the flying monkeys put in an appearance, Taz had leaned forward, totally engrossed. Reed had quietly reminded him there were no such things, it was something that had been done for the movie. Taz had whispered back there actually were such things, just not there on Earth.

That had certainly given Reed pause.

Reed checked the time. It was still early, but he could smell coffee brewing so his mom had to be up, probably cooking breakfast. Reed slipped from the bed, hunting for a pair of night pants.

"What's up?" he heard Taz ask from the bed.

Reed turned to answer, but his response became tangled in his throat. Taz was sprawled on the bed, the sheet wrapped around his lower body, his multicolored hair spread out across the pillows, a sleepy look on his face. Love rose up and grabbed Reed by the throat. Taz was beautiful, and all his. How in the world had he been so lucky to end up with such a great man? What if he hadn't been at the Empire State Building that night? What if he'd never met Taz? His kitten had brought such light to his life, showed him how much of a rut he'd been in… he'd shown Reed how to enjoy life again.

"Reed?"

"Huh?" Reed stared at Taz, his thoughts whirling.

Taz grinned slightly, brushing his long hair out of his face. "I asked what's up? Maybe I should have asked if you want to come back to bed instead."

Reed felt the blush crawl up his neck. "Oh man. I would, I really would, but I smell coffee, which means Mom's up. I was just going to the bathroom…."

Taz hiked an eyebrow as Reed continued to stand there, staring. "Might want to put some pants on first."

Reed's face flamed. "Good God, that was what I was doing, but then I got distracted by you."

"Want to get more distracted?" Taz lowered the sheet, laying bare his lean, taut stomach.

Reed's mouth watered, and not just because he could smell breakfast cooking. "Oh, I'm very tempted, but we better not. Having my mom interrupt us isn't something I want to deal with."

"I guess you have a point." Taz winked, belying his words.

"What I have is a damn hard-on, you bad cat." Reed found the pair of night pants he'd been hunting, slipped them on, and dug around in his suitcase until he found the clothes he wanted to wear. "I'm going to shower now. I'll be back in a minute."

Reed hastily left the room before Taz could suggest joining him, much as he would have enjoyed that, and power walked to the bathroom, praying not to meet anyone along the way. Not while he was in this painful… condition.

Besides, he needed to focus on something other than making love to Taz. Today his dad was coming home, finally. Peyton was driving him crazy, Jacob was a constant homophobic pain in the ass, and Peter was probably more than ready for him to return and resume control of the business.

Reed showered and dressed, then made his way to the bedroom, only to find it empty. Guessing the smell of food had pulled Taz out of bed, Reed walked to the kitchen. His mom was trying to teach Taz how to cook fried eggs.

"How do you manage to break the egg without messing up that yellow part? I just don't get it." Taz was dressed in an old pair of jeans and a black T-shirt that hugged his slender form rather nicely.

"Don't hit the side of the pan quite so hard, then—"

"Oh... ouch! Something hot just hit my foot!" he announced in an aggrieved voice.

Reed looked down. Sure enough, Taz was barefoot. Reed shook his head.

"I told you to put on shoes, sweetie. That's hot grease. Here, let me—"

"I got it, Mom." Reed pulled out a kitchen chair for Taz, then urged him into it. He grabbed a napkin off the table, knelt and wiped at the splatter, then looked carefully at the skin. It was just slightly red. Didn't look too bad, could have been worse. He kissed Taz's foot before he rose and pulled up a second chair for himself and sat. "A better question is why are you cooking stuff like that?" Reed sniffed the air. "And bacon too? Not exactly a healthy breakfast. If Dad smells all this when he gets home, he'll pitch a fit."

Jeanette frowned at Reed. "I'm cooking this for you and Taz. I need to get rid of this stuff before your dad gets home. Throwing it out seems like such a waste. Besides, I'll have the kitchen cleaned well before we leave to get your dad. He'll never know."

Reed picked up the glass in front of him and sipped at the orange juice. "Ah, so that's your story. I guess you don't plan to eat any of this yourself, huh? Since it's just for me and Taz."

Jeanette pointed a spoon at Reed. "Oh hush, you. That's my story, and I'm sticking to it."

"Good morning!"

"Here comes trouble," Reed huffed, listening to his sister clomp down the hallway.

"And yes, Renee is eating with us, and she likes this stuff too. Not another word, Reed." Jeanette turned back to the stove and started plating the food.

"Huh, maybe I should switch to coffee if I have to deal with her this early in the morning." Reed timed his words for just the right moment.

"Coffee?" Taz perked up.

"Ah...." Reed winced, realizing too late he'd used the wrong word.

"Oh bite me, Reed." Renee breezed into the kitchen and hurried over to her mom. "Hey, Mom, that looks good. Is Reed giving you trouble?"

"Oh, no more than normal," Jeanette said as Renee hugged her.

"Mmm, that looks scrumptious. I'm starved! What are you feeding Reed?" She stuck her tongue out at her brother who responded in kind.

"Don't worry, Renee," Taz hastened to reassure her. "Reed doesn't really bite hard, he—"

"Can I help with that?" Reed jumped up, before Taz could say anything else incriminating. Renee snickered, focusing on Taz.

"What's wrong with your foot?"

"Hot grease," he solemnly informed her. She nodded in sympathy.

"You have to be careful with that stuff. That's why it's not good to fry things when you're in the nude."

Before Taz could make any further inquiry in that direction, Reed set a plate in front of him, then leaned in and kissed him. He knew the distraction would work, and it did. Taz switched gears, his attention on Reed's mouth instead.

"Reed and Taz sitting in a tree." Renee's voice lilted in a singsong fashion as she pulled out a chair with her foot and flopped onto it, putting her plate before her. "K-i-s-s—"

"Renee Louise Hatcher, why don't you do something useful with that mouth instead of giving Reed and Taz trouble?" Jeanette interrupted.

When Reed managed to extricate himself from Taz by diverting his attention to his food, he watched his mother bring her own plate to the table. *Thank you,* he mouthed. She winked back at him.

They decided to take Reed's car to the hospital. The backseat was ample for three adults, and Renee and Mom could fuss over Dad to their heart's content while Reed watched the road. Jacob wasn't going to be there, luckily. And he prayed that Peyton didn't show up either. This was a time for family. Not creepy stalker ex-boyfriends.

EVEN THOUGH Herb complained, a wheelchair was brought to his room, along with an explanation that it was standard hospital procedure and was necessary for insurance purposes. After a last minute meeting with the doctor, and once a cart finally arrived to carry all the flowers, Herb was ready to go. A few of the nurses even stopped by Herb's room to say good-bye. Reed left a few minutes early so he could have the car waiting by the time his father reached the entrance. Once they got everything loaded, Reed pulled away from the hospital.

"Good grief, I can't tell you how happy I am to be out of there." Herb yawned as they made their way through traffic. "First thing I'm going to do when we get home is take a shower. I smell like a hospital."

"I've smelled worse." Reed glanced in the rearview mirror, grinning.

Renee giggled from the backseat. "Haven't we all?"

Herb rolled his eyes. "Swear to God, though, that smell just soaks into your pores. After I shower I'm going to eat and take a nap. I can't *tell* you how nice it'll be not to have someone poking or prodding me, or turning on the lights in the middle of the night, or have someone down the hall yelling. God, I'm so glad to be out of there."

Reed tensed when he heard Renee cough at their father's last words, but for once, she resisted the urge to make any comment, which Reed was thankful for. He knew what she was thinking, and if she said it, he'd kill her. Good God, he couldn't think of anything more embarrassing than his parents hearing him and Taz make love. He'd stuff a pillow in Taz's mouth—or his own—if he had to, so there'd be no "yelling down the hall" as his dad put it. Conversation was light on the drive home. Reed could see his dad was tiring. When they arrived, he parked as close to the house as possible while his mom and Renee helped Herb inside. He and Taz unloaded the car and brought his dad's stuff in. He could hear the sound of running water, the shower already going.

"He didn't waste any time, huh?" Reed stood in the hall with the bag of clothes as Renee went back outside again. "Where do you want this stuff, Mom?"

"Laundry room." Jeanette wrinkled her nose. "He's right, though. Everything does smell like a hospital. I hate that smell."

Renee returned, bearing an armful of flowers. "What about these?"

"Oh, Herb really isn't into flowers, but I like them. Why don't you put them around the living room and kitchen?" Jeanette helped Renee place the various arrangements, then started a light lunch. "Are you kids eating?"

"I could eat," Taz admitted. "Can I help with anything?"

Jeanette patted Taz's cheek. "Such a sweetie. Could you fix the drinks? Renee and Reed can have the tea in the blue pitcher. The other pitcher has a sugar substitute. Use that one for Herb's drink. Oh, I forgot to check the mail yesterday. Would one of you run out there and check for me?"

"I'll do it, Mom."

"Thanks, Reed. I should have this done in just a minute."

"Okay." Reed ducked out the door. The Florida sun beat down on him like a sledgehammer of heat. As nice as the warmer weather was, he'd gotten used to the cooler temperatures up north. And speaking of up north, if things went well with his dad, maybe he and Taz could head home soon. With that pleasant thought in mind, he opened the wrought iron mailbox at the end of the drive.

Suddenly, the sun felt like it was using him for an anvil. Sweat blossomed on his skin as the temperature seemed to soar, the brightness of the outdoors magnified a thousand times. The birds' lovely songs now sounded like nails on a chalkboard... and he couldn't breathe. Where had all the oxygen gone? The pavement rolled under him, a wave that seemed to come right at him... and little black lights flashed in front of his eyes.

There was another red rose in the damn mailbox.

TEN

TAZ DUTIFULLY poured tea, as Jeanette had requested, but managed to acquire a cup of coffee for himself at Renee's playful urging, and drank it before Reed had a chance to return and object. Not that he was sure Reed would object, but he was in too much of a hurry to drink the blessed beverage to reason it all through. He'd already started on a second cup and was exploding with energy when he had his next great idea—to run outside and surprise Reed with a kiss and a hug, a combination of the warmth of the coffee and his love for Reed stealing through his veins.

He kissed both Jeanette and Renee on top of their heads. "Be right back," he assured them, rushing through the living room toward the front door, their giggles following in his wake. He made no effort to be stealthy, too exuberant for anything as banal as subtlety. He heard the screen door close behind him as his bare feet hit the sundrenched front walk. Reed stood by the street, not moving.

Good. That made him an easier target.

Taz skipped down the walk and reached for Reed. But the expression on his lover's face drew him up cold. He looked ill, his attention riveted on something inside the small metal box. Was it Taz's imagination, or did he look to be ready to fall?

Refocusing his original intention, he threw his arm about Reed's waist, as if to hold him up. "What is it, my Reed?" he asked in consternation. And then he saw the single red rose, and his brows drew together in anger. *Again? Really?*

"Another one," Reed whispered. "That son of a bitch was here."

"We have to do something about this, Reed."

"But we can't prove it. And really, even if I called the police, what am I going to say? 'Excuse me, Officer, I want to file a complaint. You see, someone left a rose in my parents' mailbox and another one on my windshield.' Ha! The cop would probably laugh. I can't prove Peyton did this. I know it's him, but we have no proof."

Taz stepped back and frowned at the mailbox. Seemed to him the human law enforcement wasn't worth a Byrianal nickel. What purpose did they serve, if they couldn't protect people? "So we do nothing?" That didn't seem like much of a solution to him.

Reed reached into the receptacle and pulled out the rose, careful not to prick himself. Leave it to Peyton to send a subliminal message, even with the flowers he sent. Red was supposed to represent love, but in this case it resembled blood more. "I don't see that we have a choice."

"I really don't like this. He's upsetting you," Taz fretted, anxiously bouncing on the balls of his feet, feeling inadequate to help Reed as he wished.

Reed carefully handed the rose to Taz and gathered the rest of the mail. "Be careful how you hold it. Don't stick yourself on the thorns. Please throw it in the trash on the way inside."

"I'd like to throw Peyton in the trash," Taz mumbled as he walked back to the house beside Reed. That was the nicest thing he could think of he'd like to do to the human. Taz lifted the trashcan's lid and dropped the rose inside.

"Well, maybe if he doesn't get a rise out of me, he'll stop. This is just a game to him."

Taz growled softly. "Games are supposed to be fun. This isn't fun."

Reed held the door for Taz. "No, this kind of game isn't fun, I agree. Don't say anything, okay, Taz? We need to keep this between us. I don't want my dad upset, especially not right now."

"I understand, Reed. I'll be careful in what I say."

Reed brushed his lips across Taz's. "Just a little while longer, then we can go home and leave all this behind."

Taz immediately brightened at the prospect. "I like your parents, but yes, I'm ready to go home."

"I bet Peter will be more than happy to see us too. Poor guy, I feel guilty, making him work so much. When we—" Reed broke off in midsentence. Taz regarded him quizzically. His attention was focused outside, so Taz turned and looked too. A vehicle had just pulled up and parked on the street, close to the mail receptacle. Two figures emerged. He recognized one as Reed's brother, and his nose wrinkled at the sight. The other was an older man, heavy set, with little hair on the top of his head. What he had was mostly behind his ears and on his upper lip. He wore a genial smile that contrasted with Jacob's surly demeanor.

"Who's that with your brother?" Taz glanced at Reed, whose own face reflected his unhappiness with his brother's sudden appearance.

"Mayor Hydethorne," he replied. "A mayor is someone in government. He's like the head of the town." Before he could add anything else, the two men had reached the porch, and the mayor was holding out his hand to Reed.

"Hello, Reed, nice to see you again. And who have we here?" He glanced at Taz curiously, but not in an unfriendly way. Taz thought he seemed nicer than Jacob, which wasn't hard to be.

"Mayor Hydethorne, this is Taz. My boyfriend. Taz, Mayor Jeremy Hydethorne."

"Nice to meet you," the mayor intoned. Taz thought he heard a faint growl from Jacob when he shook hands with Reed's mayor.

"How do you do," Taz responded politely.

"Is Herb up to visitors? I won't stay long, I promise."

"Come on in, I'll see." Reed ushered the mayor inside. Jacob ignored him, following behind Hydethorne.

"Have a seat, Jeremy." Jacob gestured toward the couch against the front windows. "I'll get Dad." He gave Reed a pointed look, rolled his eyes at Taz, and disappeared in the direction of the kitchen.

Taz didn't bother to tell him Herb wasn't there. He wished he could follow Jacob and kick his ass, but he knew that would upset his Reed, so he forced himself to curb the desire. Besides, they had guests. And Jacob would learn the truth soon enough.

Even as he thought that, Jacob came back, followed by Jeanette and Renee. As if on cue, Herb's voice could be heard. Taz turned his head to see Reed's father walking slowly down the hall. His hair looked damp, and he wore pajamas and a bathrobe. Reed hurried to his father's side, and they walked together toward the living room where everyone now milled, the mayor having risen to his feet.

"Don't tell me I owe taxes and you're here to collect?" Herb joked. His comment produced a chuckle from the mayor who also slapped his leg, although Taz wasn't sure why. But he was too busy watching Jacob to worry at that moment. Reed's brother seemed to be glaring at Taz, as if he wished he'd go away. Taz felt a low growl rumble in his throat. Reed hastily slid his arm about Taz's waist and drew him away from the source of Taz's annoyance.

"You know I have better ways of collecting debts than that!" Hydethorne laughed and slapped himself again. "No, I wanted to see how you were doing, and see if you felt up to coming to the party at the Community Center Friday night."

Herb groaned. "Clean forgot about it," he admitted. "Don't see why not—"

Assorted voices all spoke at once.

"Dad, you just got out of the hospital…."

"Herb, honestly, I don't think…."

"Are you crazy? A party?"

The only one who didn't try to dissuade Herb was Jacob, who simply grunted, "Only if you feel up to it."

Taz, who'd remained silent, gave Jacob a look, but his expression revealed nothing. *What is he up to?*

"Of course, that goes without saying," the mayor added. Taz thought he seemed more concerned about Herb's well-being than Jacob did. "You'll come too, won't you?" Taz was surprised to find that the last words were directed at Reed and himself. "There'll be good food and good people. And music and dancing…."

Taz's eyes lit up. Dancing? Did he say dancing? He gave Reed a hopeful look. Renee spoke before Reed had a chance to.

"I think you just said the magic word, Mayor, didn't he, Reed? I think they'll be there with bells on." She giggled at her brother.

Jeanette smiled before turning to Herb. "You really think you're up for it?"

"Oh tosh, Jeannie, I'm just fine. It won't kill me. Not like I'd be dancing anyway. I think it'd do everyone some good. Y'all been spending too much time in that hospital. It's time to live again."

All eyes now turned to Reed, who nodded his agreement. "Sure, Dad. As long as you're up to it."

Acting on impulse, Taz kissed Reed, expressing his happiness. No one seemed to mind, except for Jacob, who stalked from the room. Reed pinked slightly, but he didn't protest. Jeanette suggested coffee, to which everyone agreed—especially Taz—and Renee volunteered to get it. Reed and Taz followed her into the kitchen to help, and Taz couldn't help but wonder what Reed was thinking. His eyes were filled with an unreadable expression.

"Is something wrong?" he whispered in Reed's ear, careful to keep his voice low. The clatter of Renee getting down coffee mugs and spoons helped his cause. He had no wish to worry Reed's sister; he liked her too much.

"Just thinking," Reed replied. "Don't worry. I'll tell you later, okay?" Taz had to be content with that, and another kiss. When Renee handed him a fresh mug of liquid heaven, his focus shifted, and he thought he heard Reed sigh in relief.

THE REST of the week passed with no more stalker-type things happening to upset Reed. But that didn't mean he wasn't constantly waiting for the other shoe to drop. Checking the damn mail was fast becoming an unpleasant adrenaline rush. It was like free falling without a parachute. Reed dreaded walking out to the mailbox, wondering if there would be another rose waiting for him. What next? Would he find one in his breakfast cereal? Or maybe lying in wait when he pulled back the blankets to get ready for bed? Hell, he was fast getting to the point he couldn't help but jump at every little sound. And the house seemed to be full of those.

Reed remained tense, trying his best to hide that very tenseness from Taz, which of course didn't work. Taz stayed even closer than usual, doing his best to help Reed. He rubbed Reed's shoulders, held his hand, and gently stroked his back… all his energies focused on relaxing Reed. Reed appreciated all his efforts, but he was worried his family might notice something was off with him, so he did his best to act as normal as he could around them. No sense in triggering the Hatcher family defense mechanism any sooner than he had to.

Thursday rolled around. Needing to get out of the house, Reed suggested he and Taz meet Renee at her bar. In case Taz needed extra incentive to go, he mentioned to him that it just happened to be chicken wing night too. Reed thought Taz would jump for joy at that combination—food and dancing. Plus, it would get them both out of the house and away from the eyes that seemed to follow him wherever he went.

"Hey, baby, are you about ready?"

Taz checked his image one last time then turned to face Reed. "Do you think I should pull my hair back?"

Reed stepped closer and ran his hand through all that luscious hair. "Leave it down, kitten, you know I like it free. But bring a hair tie, just in case you get hot while you're dancing and want to get it off your neck."

Taz caught Reed's hand and nuzzled it. "You look good tonight, my Reed."

Reed laughed. "Me? Have you looked in the mirror? Those damn jeans are driving me crazy the way they hug your ass." Reed patted the very ass he was talking about. "You're a damn good-looking man, Taz."

Taz grabbed Reed's shirt. He sinuously stretched along his torso until his lips were plastered against Reed's. When Reed groaned, Taz broke the kiss, an earnest expression on his face. "I am yours just as you are mine. No one else's, Reed. Totally, absolutely, and completely mine. I don't care what your ex-boyfriend thinks or does, you are *mine*."

Reed buried his hands in Taz's hair, his chest heaving as he stared into Taz's eyes, drawing strength from what he saw. "You're right. I refuse to let Peyton mess with us… with me. I have you and that's all that matters to me. What happened in the past is in the past. I'm different now."

Taz rested his hands over Reed's. "That's right, Reed. Don't let him make you doubt yourself."

"Right." Reed smiled slightly. "Fuck him. Let's go have fun."

"Exactly." Taz bounced as Reed kissed him again.

Reed pulled Taz after him into the kitchen, where his mom was studying the contents of the fridge, and told her where they were going to be. Not because he felt the need to explain their movements, but from simple courtesy, so she wouldn't worry about him. No matter how old he was, she was still his mom. Then he pulled out his cell and called Renee. "Hey there, Sis. You working tonight?"

"Yeah. Actually, I'm already here. Why? Are you two thinking of stopping by?"

Reed followed Taz out of the house and to the rental. "I thought we would, yeah. In fact, Taz and I are leaving now. I just needed to get out for a while."

"Gotcha. We're getting busy, so I'll make sure I save you a table."

Reed opened the door for Taz. He held the phone away for just a moment as he kissed him softly, then watched him slide inside. After Taz buckled up, Reed walked around to the driver side, resuming the conversation. "Wow, you're that busy on a Thursday night?"

"You bet we are. We're the hottest spot in town, don't you know?" Renee chuckled. "Tell you what, I'll have you guys' drinks and wings on the table by the time you get here. One of the perks of knowing the owner."

"Sounds good. Thanks, sis. See you soon." Reed hung up and started the car.

As they pulled out of the driveway, Taz firmly clasped Reed's free hand. "We're not going to worry about anything—just going to have fun tonight."

Reed squeezed Taz's hand. "Yeah. Just you, me, and Renee. We're gonna just kick back and have some fun."

They drove in silence to the bar. Reed refused to dwell on the crap Peyton had pulled. They deserved to enjoy themselves tonight. They'd be going back to New York soon, now that his dad was well on the road to recovery, and then all this would be behind them. He could stand a few more days and, by God, he wasn't going to let that asshole ruin what time he had left with his family. He'd already made the arrangements and bought tickets for a return flight on Saturday morning. He just needed to break the news to everyone, including Taz. Mind made up, Reed felt better as he pulled into the parking lot.

"Ohhh, it looks busy tonight." Taz eyed the cars that stretched bumper to bumper around them before leaping out of theirs.

Reed had to agree that business was booming as he followed Taz to the door. "Yeah, it sure does. Guess Renee wasn't kidding when she said the place was packed. I'm glad she saved us a table now."

When Reed reached past Taz and opened the door, the sound of music greeted him first. Wave after wave of good old-fashioned rock washed over him, relaxing him. Not head-banging metal or techno crap, or the pop flavor of the day, just rock and roll. Plus it was at just the right level—not so loud people couldn't talk, thank goodness, or so soft you could barely hear it. Yeah, this was exactly what the doctor ordered.

Reed held the door open for Taz. "Kitten, head for the main bar. I'm right behind you."

Taz nodded and Reed followed him through the crowd, maintaining a hand on Taz's lower back to steer him by. He spotted

Renee about the same time she saw Taz. Waving energetically, she motioned them to follow her.

Taz grinned from ear to ear as Renee flopped down in a booth. "Hey there!"

As Renee signaled to a waitress, she grinned at Taz and Reed. "Hey guys. The food should be here in a second. I had the kitch—Ah, here we go."

Taz bounced as baskets full of food were laid on the table along with sodas. "This is the chicken wings, right?"

"Absolutely." Reed reached for one of the succulent morsels and dug in, his mouth watering. "Damn, that's good."

"Mmm," Taz moaned as he ate.

Everyone fell quiet, occupied with enjoying the delicious wings, as well as the music. When the song ended, a DJ's voice came over the radio announcing that it was now the time they'd all been waiting for—Dedication Night. He invited listeners to call in and make song requests for all the important people in their lives. Several songs played through as they ate, with dedications that ran from the just-for-laughs variety to the heavily sentimental. The dedications were as much fun as listening to the music.

"So, is this why it's so busy tonight? Because of this dedication stuff?"

Renee shrugged. "Maybe. The show runs from five to seven, and I get a lot of couples in here the same time the station does this Thursday nights. I don't know if that's got anything to do with it or not, honestly. But, the music's usually good and the atmosphere's pretty relaxed."

"Packed too," Reed observed.

Taz ate another wing and licked his fingers in appreciation. "The music is quite nice. It's not too loud, either. I don't like when it's so loud you can't talk."

Renee nodded. "Right. It's supposed to be there in the background, able to be heard, but not overpowering."

Reed took a drink of his soda. "Well, I'd say you hit the nail on the head."

The disc jockey came on the air as another song trailed off. "Okay, listeners, I got a hot one here. This next song goes out to Reed Hatcher from someone who prefers to remain anonymous. Isn't that romantic? Well, here you go, Reed! Hope you enjoy the song."

Moments later, the haunting strains of "Every Breath You Take" filled the bar. That song, that fucking song screamed across the bar, targeting him. God, he hated that damn song... hated it as much as that asshole loved it. Reed's breathing spiked as the soulful voice of the lead singer weaved the chilling words, singing the verses that spoke of watching, longing, and belonging... to someone who refused to let go.

Reed held onto the table with a death grip. His knuckles turned white as the song wrapped around him, the disturbing lyrics playing over and over. Watching... watching... everywhere... watching.... His stomach rolled and he swallowed, hard, several times. When saliva continued to flood his mouth, he grabbed his drink and gulped the cool soda frantically. He would *not* fucking throw up. Not here. And not because of Peyton.

The words of the song buzzed around him, whipping in to take small, cold bites out of his defenses. Why didn't people see that song was about stalking? What was there in the lyrics that even remotely screamed romantic? Suddenly he was back, back to that time when he had no choice. When every move he made had been watched. When nothing he did was ever right. He broke out in a cold sweat. How many times had he ended up on the wrong side of a fist for no good reason? A small moan jerked him back to the present. Had he really made that sound?

He did *not* belong to that bastard. Oh, he knew without a doubt who had dedicated the fucking song to him—Peyton. Who else?

"Reed? *Reed*!"

Reed slowly turned his head. He tried to bring his eyes into focus. What the hell? Why was everything so fuzzy?

"Reed? My Reed?"

The clamp wedged around his heart loosened as those two simple words broke the spell of that damn song. The music faded as Reed's head cleared. Reality snapped back and a lone tear trailed down his cheek. But Taz's sweet face was recognizable to him, now that the haze of tears was gone. And in Taz's eyes was an obvious anxiety. Concern for his welfare. Something Peyton had never shown and never could.

"Are you okay? Reed?"

Taz's hand cupped his cheek, his thumb wiping the tear away. The warmth against his skin grounded him. This… this was the man who loved him, the man who would never hurt him. Taz's love for him was based on trust, not fear.

Reed turned his face and nuzzled into Taz's hand. "Yeah, yeah, I'm okay… thanks to you."

Taz stared at Reed, his forehead creased in worry lines. "Do you think…?"

"Oh yeah, babe, there's no *think* about it. I *know*."

Taz slammed his fast down on the table. "That… that…."

"Son of a bitch?" Reed volunteered. Gently, he placed his hand over Taz's closed fist.

"Not the word I was looking for," Taz huffed. "What are we going to do about this? Enough is enough."

When Renee placed her hand over both Taz and Reed's, Reed remembered his sister was sitting there, listening to everything. "I'll tell you what you're going to do. You're going to explain what the fuck just happened. Anything that makes my baby brother turn that pale, break out in a sweat, and puts such a look of fucking terror on his face *will* be shared with me. So, spill it, Reed."

REED'S HALTING words washed over Taz as he explained about Peyton to his sister. Taz already knew the story and what concerned him was Reed, not his past, but his present. He refused to let go of Reed's hand, brushing his thumb across the back of it, attempting to impart as much strength as he could through the medium of his skin.

Renee remained uncharacteristically silent, her mouth seeming stuck in the open position as she listened, her eyes growing wider and wider. When Reed had finished, she sat back in her chair and gave a long low whistle.

"Wow, when Mom and Dad—"

"No!" Reed clutched at Taz's hand, panic in his voice. "They can't know... I can't tell them.... They'd be... they'd feel guilty, I know. And I can't do that to them. Please, Renee, please tell me you won't tell them right now?"

Renee glowered. "But they *should* know what kind of a guy Peyton is. They think he's such a good guy. Hell, we all thought that, me too. I had no idea that you and him... that he.... Oh shit, that's just all kinds of messed up, Reed."

"Please, Reed's sister," Taz spoke up. He actually disagreed with Reed's decision too, but it wasn't his to make, and if that was what Reed needed to have some peace of mind, then that's what he would do. Personally, he thought Peyton deserved to be outed to the whole community for the asshole he was. Hopefully, that would happen... someday.

He poured all of his emotions into the look he gave Renee, beseeching her to please not go against Reed's wishes. She started to speak, gave up, started again, then finally heaved a large sigh.

"Fine. I won't say anything. Even if I think you're making a *huge* mistake, brother."

"Maybe I am. Hell, I don't know." He ran his free hand through his hair. "But it's my mistake to make, okay?"

"Okay," she agreed, rolling her eyes in an exaggerated fashion. "You know what? If I could, I'd dedicate a song to him, the big asshole."

"Like what?" Reed lifted his glass and took a long drink of soda.

"I dunno." Renee shrugged. "Maybe 'You're So Vain'?"

Reed almost choked on his drink. He gave a small chuckle, and Taz was grateful for the sound, even if he didn't understand the joke.

"Followed by a side order of 'You're No Good'?"

"Now you got it!" Renee said enthusiastically. She leapt up and moved around the table, drawing Reed and Taz into a group embrace. She pitched her voice for them alone. "What doesn't kill you makes you stronger. Never forget that."

She kissed Reed on his cheek, then repeated the gesture on Taz before resuming her seat. Taz scooted closer to Reed, whispering in his ear, "Together we are stronger. Never forget that, Reed." Taz was rewarded for his words by a smile that seemed more like his old Reed come back again.

"You're so very right, babe," he agreed. "You're a very wise a— man," he hastily amended. He looked across the table at his sister. "Renee, I was going to tell you tomorrow, but this seems as good a time as any. We're going home."

"Home? When?"

"Saturday morning. I've already booked the flight. It's time. Hell, it's past time. Dad's doing good, and he has you and Mom. Plus, I have a business to run. Can't expect Peter to put his life on hold forever. Hey, don't look sad."

Taz turned toward Renee. Were those tears in her eyes? He reached for her hand hastily. "No, do not be sad, Renee. It's not forever. We will come back, even if we must travel on such a primitive—"

"We'll be back before you know it," Reed smoothly interjected. "And we still have tomorrow night, don't forget that. The party at the Community Center, right?"

"Right." She took a swipe at her nose, sniffling. "I just miss you, that's all. And now I've gotten to know Taz, and… well, I think you guys are awesome. Shit, if I keep on like this I'm gonna cry." She laughed. "We'll just have to make tomorrow night special, won't we? Party like it's 1999!"

"But how can we do that?" Taz asked, baffled. "I thought it was your Earth—" Taz's next words were abruptly cut off when Reed pressed their mouths together and whatever Taz had been thinking flew out of his head.

Home. To their home. The thought was intoxicating. Just like Reed. Taz couldn't wait to go home with Reed. His heart was filled with a deep love for this sexy man he loved more than anything as he kissed him in return, Renee's exaggerated sighs of satisfaction a backdrop to their love.

ELEVEN

THE SEEMINGLY endless ride home grated on Taz's nerves. After that kiss at Renee's bar, his need for his lover was slowly building, a churning in his gut. Taz gripped Reed's hand. It took everything he had not to leap across the car, wrap his arms around Reed's neck, and… and he'd better not do that in this primitive vehicle. Damn thing was almost as bad as that contraption they flew down here on. Plus, Reed would probably yell, and not in a good way.

But when he got his human back to where they were staying, he'd make him yell, and definitely in a good way. Taz growled softly. Oh. Right. They wouldn't be alone. Oh stars, he'd forgotten. While he thoroughly loved Reed's parents, he was more than ready to return to New York. The hustle and bustle—that steady throbbing heartbeat of the city—was missing here. This place was definitely quieter. Plus there were certain people he could live without.

The pace here was much slower. Taz frowned as he remembered Reed's parents lived in a community with other older humans. He preferred the apartment Reed owned. There were many humans there around Reed's age who enjoyed the same social activities they did. Taz especially liked to go dancing. But it wasn't the older people that caused his disturbance. What had really ruined their visit was Peyton. What he wouldn't give for five Earth minutes alone with the jerk.

"Hey kitten, watch the claws."

Taz caught his breath. Just thinking about Peyton had inadvertently brought his claws out. "I'm sorry. I didn't mean to. I didn't hurt you, did I?"

"Of course not. You didn't," Reed quickly replied. "I just felt them, that's all. But I know that doesn't usually happen unless you're upset, so what's going on?"

Taz fidgeted. He looked out the window, picked at an imaginary piece of fluff on his jeans.

"Babe?" Reed squeezed Taz's hand.

Taz sighed. "Nothing, really. I was just thinking how I'd like to make love with you when we get home. Then I remembered we aren't at home, we're at your parents' home. That got me to thinking about how I'm ready to go back to New York. This is a nice place, but New York suits us better, I think. Thinking about this place made me think about Peyton and how I'd like to get him alone for a short time. I guess my claws popped out when I thought of that jerk."

"Goodness, all that, huh? Know what part I liked best, though?"

Taz grinned. "The getting Peyton alone for a short time?"

Reed snorted. "Actually, no. The 'getting me alone and making love' part. There's potential there."

Taz scooted a little closer. "We'll have to be very quiet, I think."

Reed nodded, never taking his eyes off the road. "Yes. And no roaring or loud purring."

"And no loud praying, either."

Reed cut his eyes over to Taz for a second, then glanced back at the road. "Huh? Praying?"

Taz squeezed Reed's hand. "I'm talking about all the 'oh Gods' you say while you work your cock up my ass."

"Jesus Christ." Reed's free hand jumped on the steering wheel, jerking the car. Reed quickly eased the vehicle back into the appropriate lane. "Damn, Taz, are you *trying* to make me wreck?"

Taz stretched over the console and blew in Reed's ear. "Wreck, no. Get you in the mood to fuck me? Yes."

Reed sucked in a harsh breath. "Keep that up and I'll be looking for a nice, desolate road."

Taz repeated the action, whispering, "That works for me."

"Oh God—"

"See? Praying."

Reed choked out a laugh. "Funny. Babe, I'm too old to be fucking in the backseat like a kid when there's a nice, soft bed not very far from here."

Taz slumped back to his side of the car. "But... I've never done it in the backseat, my Reed. What's it like? Is it exciting? Messy? Fun?"

"Oh God—"

"Praying again?"

Reed shook his head. "I can't believe, just can't believe that I'm thinking about this. Do you know what kind of trouble we could get into if we got caught? Seriously, I mean big trouble." Reed frowned at the road. "Trouble like going-to-jail kind of trouble. Yeah, don't think that's an experience you want. Not to mention the whole alien thing, and I'm not talking the illegal kind either. It's not safe."

Taz's eyes rounded. "Your police would take us to jail?"

"Get the right kind of asshole, and yeah, he could. Not supposed to be doing that kind of stuff in public. Sorry, Taz, but the risk isn't worth drawing the authorities' attention to you. And God, I feel like an old fogey now. What next? The four o'clock senior citizens special at Denny's?" He thumped his hand against the wheel.

Taz flipped through the definitions in his translator until he found what he wanted. "Ah, an old fogey: An extremely fussy, old-fashioned, or conservative person. I don't see you this way, Reed. Careful, yes, but that's a good thing. I tend to forget I'm an alien, you know. I'm just me. I don't feel alien, and I don't think about hiding what I am. It's good that you do."

"You're my life, so you're damn straight I'm going to do whatever I need to keep you safe." Reed pulled into his parents' driveway. The lights of the car glowed brightly against the large door that led to the place where humans kept their automobiles, reminding Taz of the twin moons of Peleos. "And that's why we're going to do this in a place that keeps you safe. I'm all for excitement, but not at the cost of losing you, babe. Okay?"

Taz leaned over the console and kissed Reed on the cheek. "You're all the excitement I need. Honest. I don't need the backseat of a car or a tiny room on an unsafe air machine to make sex interesting. All I need is you. And maybe a pillow to help drown out any sounds," he added as an afterthought.

Reed snickered. "Think that can be arranged." He flicked a button on a small device that he pulled from over his head. Taz gave him a questioning look. "I borrowed Mom and Dad's garage remote. I'm going to park inside tonight. Not taking any chances on... just not taking any chances."

Taz understood and approved. Reed's despicable ex had placed something on the car before, no sense in giving him a chance to do it again. They'd be gone soon, the car would be returned to the polite lady who had let them borrow it, and all would be well once again.

And yet... and yet he couldn't help but wonder what it would be like to crouch on all fours in the backseat of this vehicle while Reed pounded into him. The thought was making him hard, and he barely restrained a whimper. He noticed the door slowly disappear from view, opening an entry into the car room. Reed slowly moved the car into the space, closing the door behind them.

Thoughts of the nice soft bed so close at hand and yet so impossibly far began to fog Taz's brain, overtaken and pushed away by the heightening desire for his Reed that was consuming him. Before Reed had a chance to move out of his seat, Taz cupped his groin and began to rub against him, a low moan forming in the back of his throat.

"Want you so much," he murmured. "Can't... fucking... wait...."

REED SHOULDN'T have been surprised at Taz's sudden maneuver. The signs had been there, after all, if he'd been paying attention to them. And truth be told, his own desire for Taz was going a bit haywire too. He wanted his kitten just as badly as Taz wanted him. Well hell, he was still young, wasn't he? Who was an old fogey? Not him. They'd never get this chance in New York since he didn't own a car. So why the hell not?

Taz's talented hand was driving him crazy. He was half afraid he'd come before they ever got started. Better a momentary cool down while they got themselves into position—were they really going to do this, here and now?—and he took the time to explain the rules to Taz: no screaming, roaring, sudden explosions. That had never happened before, but best to cover all the bases.

Besides, he was still strapped into his seat belt, and right this minute it was strangling the bejesus out of him.

"Hang on, babe, hang on." He found it hard to remove Taz's hand, but he told himself it was for the best. At Taz's crestfallen expression, he hurriedly pressed the button on the harness and snapped it back into place before leaning across toward Taz and kissing him. "No, no, sweet love, don't look like that. I want you, I really do. Yes, right here and now. Well, right there and now." He jerked his thumb toward the backseat and was rewarded with the sight of Taz's bright smile.

Was he crazy? Undoubtedly. Were they going to do this? Hell, yes.

Taz scrambled into the backseat. Reed shook his head. There was no *way* he was climbing over that seat. He wasn't a teenager and hadn't been for a long time. Things on him actually popped now when he bent them in certain ways. There were doors on a car for a reason. And Taz was a damn sight more flexible than he was.

Taz's shirt sailed over the seat, hitting Reed. "Think this would work better if you were back here with me," he grumbled.

Reed grabbed the handle, his hand slipping off twice in his rush to get out. He finally got the door open—thank God he didn't hit his parents' car that was parked next to them—and lurched out of the rental car. The interior light highlighted Taz's stripes. His kitten had his jeans undone and was struggling to get them off. Flexible didn't begin to describe Taz... and hello, there went Taz's jeans and underwear. He'd better get back there before Taz started without him.

Reed opened the back door. "Hands off that."

Taz whimpered pitifully but released his cock.

Reed slipped into the backseat and shut the door. Was there anything as sexy as the male sitting next to him, his stripes fully showing, and God, that tail should be making an appearance any time now. "Since you need something to do with those hands, unsnap me."

Reed held his breath as Taz's hands brushed against his cock. *Not going to come, not going to come. Dammit.* He was already so close, too close. His balls ached with the need to empty. And if he didn't get his jeans undone soon, his dick was going to fall off. His clothes were strangling him. Taz flipped open his zipper, parted his pants, and fished his cock out. Remnants of the air-conditioning they'd been blasting in the car caressed his naked flesh.

"Mmm," Taz hummed as he stared at what he held. "Can I...?"

Reed ran his hand over Taz's hair. "Yeah, we don't have lube, so get me good and wet. And no deep-throating, or this party's going to be over before it starts."

"Okay," Taz purred obediently, leaning over Reed's lap.

Lord, he loved that sound. Reed fought against leaning his head back as Taz wrapped one hand around the base of his cock. It was late, and his parents *should* be asleep, but he was going to keep an eye out for them, just in case. Wet heat enveloped his cock. Reed's eyes rolled back, and all thoughts of anything but Taz's mouth flew out of his head. So much for keeping watch. Jesus fuck, that tongue of Taz's should be illegal. Actually, what he was doing probably was in a lot of places. Another reason to be careful in public.

Right at that moment, though, Reed didn't care if the whole state of Florida traipsed through the garage because Taz's tongue was meandering up and down his shaft, taking its sweet time, rubbing like crazy. He was going to lose his mind, he knew it. Taz bobbed his head slowly, pausing to suck the head while his hand jacked the bottom of Reed's dick. Saliva dripped down, wetting him. Yeah, Taz was serious about getting him ready... so much so Taz was going to make him come if he wasn't careful. Taz must have thought the same thing because he pulled off and grasped the base, still leisurely stroking.

"You're good and wet, my Reed."

"Gok," Reed grunted, then cleared his throat. Fuck, Taz had sucked the ability to speak right out of him, through his cock. "I mean good. That's good. Straddle me, babe."

Taz stole a quick kiss, then swung a leg over Reed's lap, balancing himself over the cock that pointed directly up at his ass. "As sexy as I think it is to be undressed while you're still clothed, I think we might need to get your shirt out of the way." What a time for his kitten to be practical.

"Just shove it the fuck out of the way, then," Reed growled. The head of his dick brushed Taz's hole. He was going to start foaming at the mouth if he didn't get in there and damn soon. How the hell Taz was still able to make any sort of sense was beyond him. His own thought processes were shot to hell. Reed tightened his hand around Taz's slim hips and grunted when Taz finally pushed his shirt out of the way. "Taz... *please.*"

Taz impudently flicked his nipples and Reed saw stars. Another odd sound exploded out of him. He bit his lip when Taz wiggled, then began the slow descent down his shaft. The need to just sink his fingers into Taz's hips and slam him down was nearly overwhelming. He wanted to thrust. *God,* he wanted to thrust... almost more than he wanted his next breath. The only thing that stopped him was how much that would hurt his lover. That and the fact Taz would probably rip him to shreds with his claws. Which he would fucking well deserve, since they were only using spit as lube. Rough was fine, bloody wasn't cool—he knew that firsthand.

"Oh babe, God, you're so tight. Does it hurt?"

Taz slipped down a little farther. Reed felt his tail make an appearance, jerking behind him. "Burns a little, but it's not bad."

"There's that tail." Reed flexed his hands on Taz's hips. "Take your time. I want this to be good for *both* of us."

"Almost... I'm almost... there...." Taz squirmed a little more, then dropped down the rest of the way. With a sigh, he relaxed, flush against Reed's lap. Taz leaned toward Reed, gently nipping Reed's bottom lip. "Just give me a second, okay?"

Reed rubbed his hands up and down Taz's back. "Whatever you need."

Taz shifted, waited a second, then rocked back. "All right, my Reed, I think I'm ready."

"Ah, ah... fuck." Reed huffed out a breath and rested his hands back on Taz's hips. "Yeah, you're loosening up. I can feel it."

Taz lifted up just a smidgen, rotated his hips, then eased back down. "Oh yeah, I'm ready. Fuck me, Reed. Pound my ass."

Reed might have been the one who whimpered that time. He was beyond noticing or caring. His hands automatically reclaimed Taz's hips as he leveraged himself, bracing his legs to give him the force he needed to thrust upward, inside of Taz. Oh Lord, how hot and tight he was. Just like velvet coating his dick. This was something he knew he'd never tire of, making love to Taz. This was just... perfect.

He moved up and Taz moved down, falling into a rhythm that was choreographed in their hearts. It was hard for Reed to angle himself the way he'd like; some things were just more difficult when you topped from the bottom. Taz would have to do it himself.

"C'mon, baby," he urged, "you know how to do it. You can find your prostate, just shift a little bit."

By now, he knew Taz's insides as well as their owner did, and he could find that little bundle of nerves blindfolded. Taz shifted as directed, impaling himself more on Reed's cock. Reed was rewarded with the sweet sound of pleasure that meant he'd found it the first time.

Reed felt Taz clench his muscles even more around his cock, and he knew his time was limited. Taz's own hard dick was woefully unattended to, pressed against Reed's chest. He could feel it leaking precum and knew Taz was close too.

Reed reached between them and began to pump, which produced a yowling from his lover that Taz immediately brought down to a softer screech. At that moment, Reed was beyond caring. Taz's tail was flying about. He felt it thump against his legs, but there wasn't enough room or time to maneuver it inside of him, damn the luck. That could wait until they got home, and then....

The thought of Taz fucking him with that marvelously talented prehensile tail pushed Reed over the edge, but he had the satisfaction of feeling Taz release first, his cock spasming, jets of come streaming onto Reed's chest. Reed's orgasm quickly followed, and their moans harmonized, one with the other.

Taz collapsed onto Reed, panting. Reed pushed back damp strands of multicolored hair and kissed Taz's sweaty cheek. "Oh babe, you were awesome."

"I am nothing without you, my Reed," he said simply, and Reed thought his heart would swell up and burst. How had he ever lived without this precious man who filled his life so perfectly? He hadn't, not really. But he sure as hell would now.

Reed felt the beginning of a cramp in his back. This was not the time or place for cuddling. Plus the longer they lay here, the greater the chance of discovery. And if they should happen to fall asleep? That would be a fatal error, for sure.

"C'mon, babe, let's get inside and get to bed." He hated to move Taz, especially as he seemed perfectly comfortable, but it had to be done. Taz didn't complain. He pressed soft kisses against Reed's chest and purred.

"Tomorrow night we shall eat and drink and dance at the party, yes?"

"Yes, we shall eat and drink and dance," Reed confirmed. As Taz slid back, he stretched his legs and managed to sit, arching his back so he could zip up. "Um, I think your shirt's in the front seat."

Taz draped his body over the seat, giving Reed a rather spectacular view that he was quick to admire. Too soon, Taz pulled back, shirt in hand, a grin affixed upon his pretty face. "Got it!"

Once Taz's pants were in place, they quietly exited the car, carrying their shirts. Reed was counting on his parents being asleep, but at worst, if they were spotted, they could just say they were hot and had taken off their shirts to cool off. Maybe that would work, maybe not.

They tiptoed carefully inside the house. Reed was relieved to see that the only lights were the ones his parents left on when they retired for the night. Despite a few aching muscles, he felt pretty damn good. Taz was good for him, no question of that. Even if he got him to do things outside his normal comfort level.

He sent Taz ahead and paused at the bathroom long enough to get a warm washcloth, so they could do a quick cleanup before sleep. Tomorrow night they'd have their last hurrah in Florida, tell his family good-bye, and Saturday morning they'd be headed home.

Things were finally looking up at last.

TWELVE

REED CIRCLED the parking lot of the Hydethorne Civic Center, looking for an empty parking space. The place was packed. After another trip around the building, Reed noticed people were starting to park in the grass.

Taz craned his neck, helping hunt for a spot to park. "Wow, there are a lot of people here."

"More than I thought." Giving up, Reed pulled in next to another car in the grass. "Hope we don't all get towed."

"Why would we?"

"Parking on the grass is illegal. But by God, I'm not parking a mile away, either. At least there are others parked here with me." Reed locked the rental and walked to the front of the vehicle, waiting on Taz. "Ready?"

"Ready for what? Is there something planned besides the dance?"

Reed grinned at Taz as they made their way to the front of the town's civic center. "No. I mean are you ready for all the people that are going to be in there?"

Taz shrugged. "There's a lot of people, but the only ones I'm interested in are your family members. Why should I care about strangers?"

"Good point, kitten. Very good point. I just wanted you to be prepared for the crowd." Reed tended to forget Taz was the one who came to an alien planet—Earth—and was marooned. He was finding Taz was a lot more mature than he'd given his kitten credit for.

Reed opened the door for Taz. Signs and balloons pointed the way to the dance. Following the line of people, they entered the community center. He noticed a number of in-house staff members who looked to be efficiently handling everyone's food and drink needs. Long tables packed with food were set up at the back of the room. The lighting was soft, the sound system excellent. There were round tables arranged about the perimeter, draped in gold and black cloth. The music wasn't exactly to his taste—it was what his dad called Big Band. But he'd also heard worse—he wasn't exactly a fan of rap.

"This is nice," Taz whispered to Reed, looking around. "Fancy."

"It is." Reed spotted his parents at a table across the room. "It'll probably loosen up later once the older folks head out. For now, this music's for them."

Taz bobbed his head, swaying slightly. "I kind of like it. It has a neat beat."

Reed groaned. He'd grown up listening to that stuff and really didn't care for it. "Come on, let's go sit with Mom and Dad."

Taz was still swaying to the beat as they made their way across the hall. Reed had to pull his eyes away from the sight of that totally delectable ass and to his family. No way he was going to make a spectacle of himself here. Just a few more hours to be respectable. Reed's sister sat at the table with his parents and grinned at them as they approached.

"Hey, guys." Reed bent down and hugged his mom.

"Oh good, we were hoping you'd get here early enough to visit with us." Jeanette grinned at Taz. "Looks like we might have a convert here, Herb."

"Hey, Dad." Reed shook hands with his father.

"Hey, son. Glad you got here." Herb turned to look at Taz. "So, Taz, you like this kind of music, huh?"

Taz nodded, toes tapping to the beat. "I do. I've never heard anything quite like this."

Renee goggled at Taz. "Really? You actually like this stuff? Reed? What did you do with our boy?"

"*Our* boy?" Reed mumbled, glaring at Renee. "*My* boy, don't you mean?"

Renee smirked. "Your boy, our boy—same thing."

Reed rolled his eyes. "No, you're wrong there. This isn't what's mine is yours. Besides, you aren't fooling anyone, you're just in lust with his hair."

"Got that right." Renee sighed, reaching for Taz's multicolored strands. Reed swatted her hand away and playfully growled. Taz just giggled.

Herb stood. "I'm going to get dessert. That is, unless you need me to referee?" Reed could see a twinkle in his dad's eyes that belied his words. "I have an idea. Why don't you kids get something to eat and join us?"

"Make sure that's a *small* dessert," Jeanette admonished before she grabbed Taz's hand. "Since you like the music, want to dance with me? Herb's getting tired. Reed could fix you a plate."

Taz nibbled his lips. "I don't know the dance."

"It's not hard. Please, Taz? Reed won't dance to this music."

Taz looked at Reed, amazed. "You won't dance with your mom? Shame on you. Please bring me back something to eat while I dance with your esteemed mother." Taz shook his head. "I'd be more than happy to dance with her."

Reed hiked an eyebrow, but he didn't say anything. There was really nothing to say.

Renee grinned as she watched Taz follow Jeanette onto the dance floor. "Should I tell him Mom just guilt-tripped him, or do you want to?"

Reed smiled at the retreating couple. "Naw. Let them be. Mom has someone to dance with, and Taz likes this kind of music."

Herb gestured to the tables at the back of the room. "And I'm thankful he's willing to dance with your mom. I just can't cut a rug like I used to."

Reed patted his dad on the back. "You will, just give it some time, Dad. Now, where's the food? I'm hungry."

"Some things never change," Renee huffed.

"Like your smart mouth?"

"Kids," Herb mumbled as they walked to the serving table. It was buried under all kinds of food. "Don't make me get your mom."

Both Reed and Renee buttoned it.

"It's amazing how that works even now," Herb gloated as he grabbed a clean plate.

Reed didn't say anything, just winked at Renee as he piled food onto two plates, carefully balancing them as he made selections from the cornucopia in front of them.

Renee filled her own plate and added a roll. "So, Dad, is Jacob coming?"

"As far as I know, he is."

"Lovely," Reed muttered, turning from the table.

"He'll behave." Herb followed Reed.

"How do you know that?"

"Because I talked to him last night and told him the fighting between you and him was stressing me out. Stress isn't good for me right now, you know. Could cause all sorts of problems, and let's not forget I just got out of the hospital." Herb laughed as he sat. "I can guilt folks as good as your mom, don't think I can't."

"Dad!" Reed snorted.

"Son, I learned it from a master. Jacob will act right, trust me."

"As long as he acts human, that's all I care about," Renee added.

Reed jerked. Of all the things she could've said. Reed hoped Jacob wasn't the only one acting human tonight.

Just then, Mom and Taz returned from the dance floor, arm in arm. Reed noticed his mother's face was flushed and she was visibly glowing. He was so happy Taz got along very well with his parents. Love for his kitten filled his heart.

Taz escorted Reed's mom to her seat then returned to Reed, leaning down and kissing him softly before turning his attention to the food at his place. He plopped into his chair and inhaled the delicious aroma before digging in with great gusto.

Nobody spoke for a few minutes as the repast was enjoyed. Finally, Reed cleared his throat, and everybody looked at him expectantly.

"This is as good a time as any to tell you that Taz and I are going home tomorrow."

"Tomorrow?" His mom paused in the act of reaching for her coffee. Renee began to pout.

"Already?" she whined. Reed could feel her gearing up for a temper tantrum.

"I did tell you that, remember?" he pointed out, trying to keep her grumbling to a minimum.

"Don't be selfish." His father unexpectedly came to his rescue. "The man has a business to run. I'm doing just fine, aren't I? I'm well out of the woods. I'm sure Reed and Taz would like to sleep in their own bed too. Visiting is fine, but there's no place like home, am I right, son?"

Reed was overwhelmed with love for his father. He'd never realized before just what a good man his father was. To have him not only understand his son's business dilemma, but to appreciate his needs. Well, it felt damn good. His dad was proud of him, and it showed.

"Yeah, you're so right, Dad." He gulped down a lump in his throat and reached for Taz's hand, squeezing it silently.

"I'd say this calls for a toast, what do you think?" Herb looked around the table.

"I'm out," Reed began to say, but Taz hastily interjected, "I know where the barman is. I will get us each one."

Reed wanted to protest, but he realized Taz was a fully grown... alien and he'd come all the way to Earth from a distant planet. Surely he could handle getting a couple of drinks? "Sure. Thanks, baby." He was rewarded with a big smile from Taz, and another kiss, before he left the table.

TAZ REMEMBERED the name of the beverages they were drinking—he and Reed had ordered them before in New York, and he'd made a point of learning what they were because they were so tasty. *Margarita.* He repeated the word to himself as he fairly skipped across the floor to the bar. He felt wonderful. Here they were, enjoying themselves with Reed's wonderful family, eating delicious food, drinking yummy drinks, and dancing! And on top of all that, tomorrow they were going home. Life was very good indeed. His only regret was not being able to contact his family to tell them he was fine, but he hoped to solve that difficulty soon.

The bar was fairly deserted as Taz approached. The barman wiped down the bar with a towel. He looked up at Taz with a smile. "What can I get for you?" he asked.

"Two margaritas," Taz ordered.

"Be right back. I was just about to get some more limes from the kitchen. Lot of tequila drinkers tonight." He winked at Taz and came around from behind the bar, disappearing quickly from view. Taz didn't mind. He leaned his elbows on the newly clean surface of the bar and gazed in admiration at the color, size, and shape of the various bottles on display before him. He was especially fascinated by a blue liquid that reminded him of a drink on his home planet of Trygos.

He heard a noise just beside him, like someone had cleared his throat. He casually glanced over, expecting to see another happy partygoer, then frowned. It was Peyton Wheeler who stood there. Reed's horrible ex. He wanted to hit him so badly, to scream and yell at him for the things he'd done to Taz's Reed. But he knew that would make Reed unhappy, so he held himself in check and decided to ignore the other man.

Unfortunately, Wheeler wasn't going to make it quite that easy.

He was staring down at something in his hands. Taz looked away, but he couldn't ignore the irritating voice.

"You think he's something now, you should have seen him when I had him," Peyton said. "He did everything I wanted. He was a good sub, knew his place. And he loved the way I dominated him. Told me there could never be anyone better than me."

Taz drummed his fingers against the bar and held his tongue.

"So, I hear you're going home, are you? Well, all I have to do is snap my fingers"—Taz heard a sound, as if Peyton were demonstrating his ability to do just that, but he refused to look—"and Reed would be mine again."

Something slid in front of Taz on the bar. Startled, he glanced down. It was indeed a photograph. In the picture were Reed and Peyton, obviously taken a few years before. They looked rather cozy.

"His heart's still mine," Peyton insisted. "He's just pretending with you. Don't you think I know the difference?"

At that moment, the bartender returned. "Sorry about that," he apologized. "Two margaritas coming right up. Be right with you." That was aimed at Peyton.

Taz pushed the photograph back toward Peyton. This man did not impress him in the slightest. In his experience, those who bragged about how great they were generally weren't. Like Vorlod. The bartender placed the drinks on the bar, and Taz picked them up.

"Thank you very much," he said before turning toward Peyton. There were so many things he wanted to say, but he left it at, "You are a fool," and walked away, back toward Reed.

He returned to the table. Reed sat there, smiling at something Renee had said while Herb and Jeanette were talking to another couple who stood beside them. He found it hard to believe Reed was submissive, at least not according to the definition supplied to him by the translator. Reed was far too strong-willed. The man ran a business and handled all the requisite problems that came with it. He had employees, charts, shipping orders, and spreadsheets he balanced with no problems. What was it Peyton said? Something about Reed knowing his place?

That Peyton could say that and mean it was bothersome to Taz. Taz knew Reed wasn't truly submissive, he'd seen that firsthand. While he didn't understand why Reed had stayed as long as he did with Peyton, he did understand how fear could immobilize a person. He did understand about a lack of self-confidence. Wasn't that part of his own situation with Vorlod? He hadn't believed in himself enough to see what a creep Vorlod really was. Taz and Reed had talked at length about Reed's past with Peyton, and frankly, Taz thought Peyton was nothing more than a bully. Yes, bullies seemed to be universal.

"Are you okay?"

Taz focused his attention on Reed. Should he tell Reed what Peyton said to him? He had a right to know, and Taz had no wish to be less than honest with him. He glanced around the table. Not a good time. There were too many people and not enough privacy. He knew how Reed felt about having others hear things about him that he considered private. "I'm fine. I was just thinking about us." Which was partially true. He would rectify his sin of omission later.

"Oh. I was just wondering. You had this funny look on your face."

"Being here with you and your wonderful parents… I miss mine, Reed, that's all. But I have to say I'm ready to go home too. I miss our life."

"Me too."

Time to change the subject. He was afraid if they continued in this vein, he'd end up crying, and that would not do at all. This was a party; it should be a happy occasion, not a sorrowful one. That gave him an idea. "Want to dance?"

"I'd love to, babe," Reed replied, his voice filled with regret, "but I think we better not. That might be pushing our relationship in the natives' faces a bit much. Last thing I want to do is get in a fight, or have someone say something that might upset my parents… and dammit, speak of the devil."

Taz quickly looked around. There was a devil here? "Where?"

"It's Jacob. I mean I see Jacob. And he's making his way over here, of course. Guess it was too much to hope he wouldn't really show up. Hopefully he won't make any snide comments, and he'll behave like Dad said he would."

Renee leaned forward. "Hope springs eternal, doesn't it, bro?"

Reed snorted. "Just leave him alone. As much as I dislike him, I guess he has every right to be here. Probably more so than me."

Renee swatted Reed's arm. "Now why in God's name would you say that? And you better hope Mom doesn't hear you say that either."

Reed stared at the tablecloth. "He lives in this area. He's here all the time, and he does things for Mom and Dad. I don't come down near often enough."

"Yeah, about that. They don't know why you moved all the way to New York. If they did—"

Reed jerked his eyes up and glared at Renee. "Oh no, not going there, Renee. Just not. It's over, and there's no reason for them to know about something I'd just as soon they didn't know about, if you get my drift. Older brother included. Not that he'd care. Knowing Jacob, he'd blame the whole awful situation on me somehow."

Renee frowned. "Well, he's a turd."

Taz had been silently following the exchange between Reed and his sister. Suddenly he snickered. "A… a lump of excrement. A log-shaped piece of shit. Also called scat or dung. Oh stars, that's perfect! I must remember that."

Renee's laughter rang loud. "What are you? Mr. Wikipedia?"

Reed covered Taz's hand, shaking his head slightly. Okay, so yes, Taz had been translating the word aloud. He hadn't meant to, but it was a good word, one Taz hoped to use on his own brother one day. Although he wasn't the jackass Reed's brother was, Cal had the capacity to act like a turd himself.

Jacob joined them, a small frown tugging at his lips. But he didn't make any homophobic comments, which was a relief to Taz. Not that it seemed to matter. As soon as Jacob sat at the table, a blanket of unease covered the group. Everyone was nervous, just waiting for Jacob to say or do something. It was so bad, Taz just wished he'd go on and do it so they could all move on.

Finally Renee had enough and grabbed Taz by the hand. "Let's dance."

Taz glanced at Reed.

"Go ahead, babe. You love to dance, and Renee's an excellent dancer."

A smile, a quick wink, and a breath of relief. Taz followed Renee to the dance floor. Reed was right, she was a good dancer. The music had a good strong beat, one Reed had said was more their generation. Whatever that meant.

HIS PARENTS were certainly popular. Now they were talking to another couple who'd approached the table, inquiring after his dad's health, so that left him and Jacob to make small talk. Yeah, he'd rather have a tooth pulled with no pain medicine. He picked up a spoon and idly drummed it on the tabletop, both to annoy his brother and to avoid dealing with him. Taz and Renee weren't coming back anytime soon, he'd bet, now that his kitten was stretching his beautiful legs on the dance floor, and his parents were deep in conversation with that other couple. Right. Trip to get food or a trip to the restroom. One or the other because he damn sure wasn't sitting here with Jacob, waiting for the other shoe to drop.

"I'll be back." He'd have done the Terminator accent if he thought Jacob would get it. He probably wouldn't, so he'd only end up looking like a dork. More of a dork. Whatever.

Reed stood. For a moment he considered explaining himself, but then he decided to hell with it and headed for the restroom. Besides, this was probably smarter than waiting for Taz to come back, since he tended to have inappropriate thoughts in public places. Like men's rooms.

As he walked in, he saw an older man drying his hands at one of the sinks. He nodded to Reed, who nodded back. The door creaked as the other man left the room. Now he was alone. He stood for a moment, staring into his reflection, lost in thought as he tried to remember a time when he and Jacob hadn't stood on opposite sides of the fence. He couldn't think of one to save his life.

The door creaked again, but Reed didn't bother to look. Until a familiar voice sent unpleasant chills along his spine. He repressed a shudder at the sound.

"I honestly don't know what you see in him." Peyton took up a position by the other sink, standing too close to Reed for his liking. Peyton pulled a comb from his pocket and began to run it through his hair. "Oh he's pretty, I'll grant you that. Dumb as a bag of hammers too. Funny, I thought you preferred someone with a little more brains, you know?" He gave an inelegant snort.

Reed clenched his fists. He wasn't going to listen to this, no way. And he wasn't going to respond. It wouldn't do any good anyway. He was and always had been powerless against Peyton Wheeler. That's why he'd been in such a horrible position. Damned if he was going to let that happen again.

He turned to leave, but Peyton moved more quickly, blocking his way. "I didn't say you could leave," he said in a deceptively soft voice, one Reed was only too familiar with. Memories flooded his brain and not good ones at that. He felt his insides churn in the familiar pattern of weakness.

"No one can be as good for you as me and you know it." He placed one firm hand on Reed's shoulder. "You never had it so good as when you were with me, admit it."

Reed found his voice, but it sounded funny even to his own ears. "I... I won't. Admit it. I mean, it's not true." Dammit, was that the best he could do?

Peyton reached out, tracing Reed's cheek with one finger. When Reed attempted to shake him off, he leaned in, holding his hand against Reed's cheek as he murmured, "Bet you miss my cock inside your ass. Never had it so good, not like I gave, did you? Who knows how you like it the way I do? Who's your Dom? I am, and you know it. That scrawny thing could never be the man I am. You need me, Reed, need me to fuck you back into my life. Send him packing to New York, and let's you and me pick up where we left off."

Where the fuck was this even coming from? To Reed's horror, he saw Peyton closing in for the kill, his mouth closing in on Reed's. Reed froze, like a deer in headlights, unable to think or move....

TAZ HAD danced a couple of dances with Reed's sister, and he was having a blast, so much so that he wanted to share it with Reed. But when he looked over at the table, he saw that Reed wasn't back yet. Odd. How long did it take him to go to the bathroom? And then a thought tickled Taz's brain, and he began to smile.

Of course. Reed was waiting for him there. Waiting for things that could not be done in public. *Oh yes, Reed, coming*, he thought. "Um, Renee? Gotta go," he told her, walking her quickly from the dance floor, back toward the table.

"Hey, where's the fire?" She laughed.

He started to ask why she thought there was a fire, but pushed the thought aside and mumbled, "Gotta go," and hurried in the direction he knew Reed had gone.

The first thing he saw when he opened the door was Reed, his back to him. But then the next second he realized who stood beside him, and who was touching him, and a fierce growl rose from him.

"Let go of him," he commanded, surprised at how calm he sounded when what he really wanted to do was tear Peyton's head off. Reed turned toward him, and he saw the utter fear and shame in his eyes. His desire to kill Peyton grew stronger. How dare he do this to Reed?

How dare he?

He and Reed stared at one another, and it seemed as though something changed, as if Reed drew strength from his presence. He knew this was Reed's fight and always had been. Common sense told him he had to let Reed handle it himself. But Taz could be here for him, in case Reed needed him. Not ripping Peyton's throat out was the hardest thing he'd ever had to do, but Taz knew it was the right thing.

"You can do this," he told Reed in a quiet voice. "You can walk away from him." And he held out his hand to his lover. "I'm here, I am yours…."

THIRTEEN

FREEDOM RACED through Reed's veins, the rush leaving him slightly lightheaded as he stared at the hand held out to him. Taz only wanted him. He wasn't interested in pushing him, belittling him, punishing him. Taz didn't need to have him begging on the floor, wouldn't call him names. No, Taz truly loved him. Taz wanted to share the laughter, the grins, the tears. Taz just wanted *him*—and all the good, bad, and ugly that went with him.

Taz made him feel alive... whole. Loved. There were no sudden slaps, mean words, or rough sex. He didn't need Peyton. God, the very last thing he needed was Peyton, and damned if he was going to fall back in that trap. It had taken time, and a whole lot of soul searching, but he'd finally found his courage and left Peyton behind.

It'd been one of the hardest things he'd ever done. Leaving his family was bad enough. Moving all the way across the country to New York had struck terror in his heart. But he'd done it. Not only done it, but achieved what he wanted. He'd opened a business and made it damn successful. Fuck Peyton, he wasn't a screwup.

"Reed? I said send lover boy there back to New York. We'll pick up where we left off. You need *me*."

"Reed?" Taz whispered.

Peyton made him feel worthless, dirty... Taz made him *feel*. Feel all the good and bad things life had to offer. Taz made a point of being there to help him deal with it. They were together, a couple. They handled life's little unpleasantries as one. Taz didn't make him doubt himself. No, Taz was the one he needed.

Reed took Taz's hand. "You're wrong, Peyton. Wrong about a lot of things but mainly about me. I don't need you. I never did, I just couldn't see that for the longest time. I'm not submissive and never was, but you couldn't see that. No, actually, you wouldn't *listen* when I told you. It wasn't what you wanted to hear. And arguing with you ended up with me having a bloody lip. You wanted to own me, run my life. And that would've been fine if that's what I'd wanted too."

Peyton crossed his arms over his chest. "You didn't know what you wanted or what was good for you. You still don't."

"I damn sure know verbal abuse isn't good for me." Reed's voice rose. "Or the hits I took. I never knew if I was going to get a kind word or the back of your hand. I wasn't submissive, I was intimidated. Big fucking difference. I didn't enjoy what we did, but you wouldn't *listen*. The more I fought you and your ways, the more you destroyed my confidence. I was afraid of you. Ashamed. That's not a Dom/sub relationship. *That's* an abusive relationship."

Taz glared at Peyton. "You tell him, Reed."

"And damned if I didn't nearly let you do it again. I let you intimidate me, let the old memories and insecurity haunt me... the shame tear at me." Reed stepped closer to Peyton, his fist clenched. "No more. You're nothing but a bully. And I'm done being a victim. You don't have any power over me anymore, Peyton, because I refuse to give it to you."

"You sure about that?" Peyton's hand swung up, aimed at Reed's face.

Taz snarled, unable to stop himself. He dropped Reed's hand, reaching out to grab Peyton's hand....

Reed caught Peyton's wrist just as Taz grabbed Peyton's arm. "Yeah, I don't think so. You see? Taz and I work together. He looks out for me, and I look out for him. We're equals."

"Something you have no understanding of," Taz growled.

Reed suddenly smiled. "And trust me when I say if I let him loose on you, you'd be on the losing end. You have no idea what you're messing with here."

"He doesn't scare me." Peyton jerked his hand away. "He's nothing, just useless, stupid fluff."

Reed laughed, actually laughed at Peyton, something he'd never dared to do before. "You're the stupid one."

Peyton tightened his mouth and narrowed his eyes. "You dare? I'll show you—"

Taz went to step forward. "Oh, please do—"

"Fuck…." Reed had an image of them rolling around on the restroom floor with his mom standing over them yelling. "Peyton, just stop this crap and—"

The restroom door opened and in walked Jacob.

All three men stared at the newcomer. Reed's stomach sank to his knees. Of all the people who could have walked in, it had to be his asshole brother. "Jesus Christ, can this get any fucking worse?"

Jacob frowned at Reed. "Stop using the Lord's name in vain. And what's going on in here? Why are the three of you just standing around? Oh, no. Surely you wouldn't…. Please tell me you weren't doing some sleazy gay thing in here, Reed."

"I'm not the one you should be worried about doing sleazy gay things, Jacob," Reed snapped, then cringed.

"What does that mean?"

"Nothing. Just forget it, Jacob. Let's go, Taz," Reed mumbled.

Taz grabbed Reed's arm. "Reed? It's time, don't you think? I'll stand with you, you know that."

Reed looked at Taz. "I would, I swear I would, but it won't do any good. Besides, there's no proof. Jacob won't take my word for anything."

"If you want to do this, then there *is* a way to prove it. Right here and right now. If you really want to…."

Reed hesitated. "There is?"

"Yes."

Reed blew out a hard breath. "Good. Then yeah, do it. I'm tired of hiding."

Taz turned to look at Jacob. "Peyton has a photo. You think Peyton is so great? You think he's as anti-gay as you? Ask him to show you the picture he has of him and Reed from several years ago. He has it in his pocket. Did you know they were in a relationship? A bad relationship? Will you care about the fact that Peyton was abusive to your brother? And Reed was ashamed. So much so that he hid the abuse and the relationship from his family. That's the reason why your brother moved all the way to New York City. He knew you'd never understand or support him."

Jacob stared at them with his mouth gaping. He looked first at Reed then Peyton. "No way. I... I... there's no way. Let me see this picture, Peyton."

Reed could practically watch the wheels turn in Peyton's feeble brain as he tried to bluff his way out of the situation. He didn't know how Taz knew about the photo, but he sure as shit believed him. He set his lips in a firm line, meeting Peyton's almost desperate glance. *No, not this time, mister. Time for show and tell.* Let's see him explain this away to his good friend and fellow homophobe, brother Jacob.

Jacob held out his hand. Peyton made a show of slowly reaching into his pocket, finally pulling out a photograph. He handed it to Jacob, along with a show of bravado. "Hey, we're friends, right? Nothing wrong with getting your picture taken with a friend, is there?" Reed saw beads of sweat on Peyton's forehead. The knowledge that he and Taz were making his ex very uncomfortable filled him with great glee.

Jacob took the picture and stared at it hard for a long moment, before turning it over to Reed. Reed glanced at a piece of his old life. He winced, noticing a bruise along one cheek. He vaguely remembered getting slapped, hard—for what, he no longer remembered. Afterward, Peyton had taken him out somewhere, even though Reed hadn't been in the mood to go. They'd ended up in a little photo booth and Peyton insisted on getting their picture taken.

His warped way of proving that all was right in their crazy fucked-up world.

"Tell me the truth, Reed." Jacob's voice was stern, yet not unreasonable. Reed clutched at the small hope that his brother might believe him. He drew in a breath and responded with more strength than he would have believed possible a short time earlier.

"The truth is we were once a couple in every sense of the word. And he was abusive...."

"Abusive?" Peyton scoffed. "Not what you said then—"

"Shut up!"

Reed was surprised to hear those words coming from his brother. Jacob took the photograph from Reed's hands and threw it back at Peyton. "You damn hypocrite. I can see it as plain as day. So what makes you any different than him? You're certainly not any better. In fact, you're worse."

Reed took Taz's hand. "Time to go," he said.

"Definitely," Taz agreed. Hand in hand, they left the men's room. Reed could hear Jacob and Peyton follow, but he never looked back, and he knew he never would again. Taz had given him the strength to look to the future—a future with Taz by his side. And Reed knew what he needed to do.

By the time they reached his parents' table, they were sitting there alone with Renee. Good, just the opportunity he needed.

"Is something wrong, dear?" his mother asked. She was always the intuitive one, and her concern drew a small smile of reassurance from him.

"No, not anymore. Look, I have to tell you something. Something I shoulda told you a long time ago." He and Taz took seats near his mom and dad, and Reed began to speak.

"I know you support me and have ever since I came out to you. But what I could never tell you was that... well, I was in an abusive relationship... with Peyton... and I let him do things to me I'm not proud of. I let him strip me of my dignity and my self-worth. I let him treat me like I was nothing and no one, and when it got too bad I ran to New York to get away from him. I had no idea he'd end up a part of your life, or I would have said something before...."

All eyes swiveled toward Jacob and Peyton as they approached the table. Jacob stepped away from Peyton, and that spoke volumes to Reed. Peyton threw up his hands in protest. "Look, I think there's been a mistake here."

"Yeah, and you made it," Renee growled, jumping to Reed's defense.

Reed was afraid to look at his parents, afraid of... what? Pity? Censure? Disgust? But when he finally dared to glance at them, all he saw was love for him, and indignation for what he'd suffered.

"Peyton, is this true?" his dad asked in a no-nonsense voice. Reed watched Peyton visibly quail. Nice to see the tables turned for once. Although he would have liked to have seen Taz have a go at him. But this way was really better.

"What's true is that Reed doesn't realize what he's given up. I'm the best thing that ever happened to him," he blustered, but Reed could see he wasn't sure of himself, not at all, and the knowledge gave him great pleasure.

"You should go now, Peyton." That was his mother. She was too much of a lady, he knew, to do anything in public, but he could see that she was angry, and it wouldn't take much for her to snap.

"Go away, Peyton," he seconded her words, and everyone else at the table added their voices in a growing unison. Peyton hovered for a moment, before turning and skulking away.

Reed's mother came around the table and hugged him. "I'm so sorry," she murmured. "If we'd only known.... Honey, I don't know what to say. We were wrong about him. I'm sorry for what he did to you."

Reed rested his head against his mother for just a moment. "Thanks, Mom." From the corner of his eye, he saw Taz's smile of encouragement, the warmth in his lover's eyes. He rose from the table, cleared his throat as he looked around at all of them before focusing his attention on Taz.

"Taz saved me from him," he said. "Taz made me realize I'm a better man than I thought I was. He healed me with his love." Suddenly he dropped to one knee in front of Taz, looking up at him in earnest.

"Taz, you are the best thing that has ever happened to me. You dropped into my life out of the blue, but it was no accident. I believe we were meant to meet, meant to fall in love, and meant to be together. I never want to be without you, ever again. For you are mine as I am yours. Taz, will you please marry me and live with me for the rest of our lives?"

"Oh my stars, oh my stars!" Taz's hand flew to his mouth. His eyes suddenly burned with unleashed tears. He stood frozen, staring in shock at Reed.

Reed grinned up at the man who stood as still as a statue—a rare state for Taz. Hell, even the music had stopped and silence filled the room. And as much as he enjoyed the look of stunned pleasure on his lover's face, the floor was getting rather hard on his knee. "Is that a yes, Taz?"

"Oh my stars, Reed! Yes, yes, yes!" Taz bounced onto his toes, giggling wildly. Then he threw himself down on the ground too and grabbed Reed's hands.

"Ah… babe, you didn't have to—"

Solemnly, Taz stared back at Reed, both of them on their knees. "You are mine and I am yours. Yes, I will marry you." Taz brushed his lips across Reed's.

"Oh my gosh." Jeanette sobbed quietly, clutching Herb's hand. "My baby is getting married."

"And we're getting another son," Herb said.

"About damn time," Renee complained. "I swear, I've never seen two people more in love."

Reed stood and helped Taz up, then hugged his mom. Jeanette threw her arms around Reed, the tears flowing swiftly. "Thank you for doing that here. You have no idea what seeing you ask the man you love to marry you means to me." Jeanette pulled back and looked at Reed. "I love you, baby. Now, we have a wedding to plan."

Reed groaned.

"Oh goodie." Renee gleefully rubbed her hands together. "This is going to be so much fun since it's you and not me!"

Taz poked Renee in the arm. "You're next."

Renee shook her head. "Yeah, right. There's no way that's happening." She snorted at the idea.

Jeanette tugged Reed's sleeve. "Before you leave we need to talk colors, flowers, dates, places, music…."

"Liquor," Herb added.

"Too bad you can't have any." Renee smirked, shoulder bumping her dad.

"Says you," Herb countered.

"Actually, says me," Jeanette added. "Well, maybe a glass. If you eat how you're supposed to in the meantime."

Reed grinned at the look on his dad's face. Time to get the focus off Dad; he was turning red. "Mom, we have time. Taz and I haven't even set a date."

Jeanette turned her attention to Reed. "All I ask is that you wait long enough for your dad to be able to fly up there. There's no way we're missing this. I know there isn't much I can do since I live so far away, but I can do some things."

"Yes, you can. I know what this means to you, so have at it."

Taz hugged Jeanette. "We welcome any ideas you have."

Jacob cleared his throat and the entire family went quiet. Reed frowned at Jacob. He'd noticed Jacob hadn't spoken. Surely his brother wouldn't ruin this for him?

Jacob shifted from foot to foot then held out his hand. "Congratulations. I wish you both much happiness."

Reed's mouth dropped open in shock, but he quickly got it shut and took Jacob's hand. "Thank you."

"I…. What Peyton did was wrong. Abuse is abuse, and I feel strongly about that. That my own brother went through such—" Jacob gulped. "And I didn't know…. That bothers me. And I didn't know because I shut you out. I… took a good hard look at Peyton and saw myself. I didn't like that. I was as bad as Peyton to you, just in a different way. I'm sorry for that. I still feel what you do is a sin, but the way I treated you is a sin too. I see that now."

"Wow. I'm shocked."

"I'm trying, Reed."

Reed pulled his brother into a quick hug. "That's all I can ask."

Jeanette patted both of her sons on the back. "You boys have made me very happy. So, Reed, what colors do you and Taz like? And you boys should work on picking a date too. And Reed? I need to make sure I have a current e-mail address for you. We're going to be talking... a lot."

"Aw, man."

At Taz's infectious giggle, the whole family laughed.

LESS THAN twenty-four hours later, Reed and Taz were outside their apartment building in New York City. It was late afternoon, and Reed had just paid the taxi driver. What a relief. He took his change and turned back in time to see Taz zip up his jacket and bury his hands in his pockets.

"I bet you're cold," Reed sympathized as Taz nodded. He wondered what the climate on Taz's planet was like. He was used to New York himself and didn't notice it quite as much as when he'd first arrived. He was a New Yorker now, and he liked it.

"Let's get you inside." Reed led him up to their apartment. They had a ton of stuff to do. The first thing was to unpack. Then he needed to call Peter. Poor guy was probably ready for a break. He felt guilty for laying such a burden on him, even if he kept saying he didn't mind. They also had a bunch of clothes to wash, since he'd refused to put the burden of their dirty laundry on his mom. He heard Taz's stomach growl. Oh, and they also needed to buy groceries. They hadn't left enough in the fridge to feed a gnat. Better add eating to the list of things to do.

"Hungry, babe?"

"I would love to eat."

Reed had to smile. He loved being able to read Taz so well, at least in that respect.

"Want to go out or order in?"

"We just got here." Taz glanced at the apartment. "I'd like to stay in, if you don't mind. Don't take this the wrong way, but I'm a little tired of humans. Between the ride to the airport there, the flight home, the airport here, then the ride here…. Humans can be very rude, I have to say…."

Reed winked. "I hope you're not tired of *all* humans."

Taz bounced across the room and threw his arms around Reed's neck. "I never get tired of *you*, my Reed."

Reed hugged Taz, lifting him off his feet for a second. "Good Lord, where do you get the energy, kitten?"

Taz hugged back, a soft purr filling the air, as he rubbed his cheek against Reed's chin. "I'm just so glad to be home. I can be myself now."

Reed lowered Taz to his feet. "Yeah, you can. I know it's not easy for you, hiding so much of your nature."

"It's what I have to do to be with you." Taz lightly shrugged. "Besides, it's nothing we can change, so don't worry about it." Taz perked up. "What's for dinner?"

Reed planted a kiss on Taz's cheek then stepped away. "How about Chinese? And turn the heat up a little, will you? I think it's a little cold in here."

"Chinese sounds good. Is the menu in the kitchen?"

"Yeah, in the junk drawer. Let's place our order then unpack." Reed looked over the menu. "After we eat, I need to call Peter and tell him we'll be in tomorrow. I need to get caught up on what's been going on while we were in Florida. So, what do you want from the Chinese place?"

"Sweet and sour chicken, for sure." Taz joined Reed in the kitchen and picked out a few more things from the menu. Reed had to smile at his bottomless pit. While Reed placed the order, Taz unpacked their clothes and started a load of laundry. It was all so very normal, so domestic, and Reed loved it. Just the two of them living an ordinary life. Nothing strange or alien to see here.

A knock at the door proved to be their neighbor across the hall. Mrs. Benson was a widow in her early sixties, and she'd lived in the building since the time of the dinosaurs, according to her. She had taken Reed under her wing when he first moved in, and had fallen under Taz's spell when he'd moved in with Reed. They were her boys, and she'd do anything for them, including picking up their mail.

Reed thanked her as he took the bundle of what was undoubtedly a lot of junk mail along with a few bills, and the key to his box. She only stayed long enough to wish them a good evening before returning to her own apartment.

Reed closed the door behind her and began thumbing through the stack. Yep, the usual. Advertisements for products he didn't want/didn't need/couldn't use. Those went straight in the trash. The bills he set aside for later. He didn't intend to spend his first night at home delving into financial matters; those could wait.

What is this? His name and address were handwritten on the envelope, so it wasn't part of a mass mailing. He frowned at the letter, debating whether or not to open it. If it was bad news, surely it could wait until tomorrow?

He glanced up as Taz entered the room with a sneeze. Reed had to smile in spite of himself. His kitten had become fascinated with the scented sheets that Reed used in the dryer. Every time he did the laundry, he would smell them, often to the point where they made him sneeze. Reed had no doubt that was the cause of this current nasal irritation.

"What's that?" Taz sniffled, pointing at the mail he still held.

"I dunno," he said before finally taking a look at the return address. Oh, him again. It had been so long, he'd almost forgotten. "Never mind, I know what it is. His name is Denby. He's been after me to buy the shop for a while. I thought he'd given up."

Of course the answer was no, but he still felt obliged to look and see what the nut job's latest offer was. Reed wasn't sure what made his shop so attractive to him. True, he did well, and he was popular among his clientele. But still…. He slid his finger beneath the flap and slid it open with practiced ease, then pulled out the contents and looked them over. He gave a long low whistle.

"Is something wrong?" Taz frowned.

"No, no," Reed hastened to reassure him, shoving the paper back inside the envelope. "He's just upped the ante pretty good. Oh well, this can wait too." He added it to the stack of bills and set it on the table. He'd get to that later.

Glancing at his watch, he decided he had time for a quick call to Peter before the food arrived, just to tell him they were back and would be in tomorrow. Peter answered on the second ring.

"A Touch of Class, this is Peter speaking, how can I help you?" It felt damn good to hear Peter's voice.

"Hey, it's me."

"Hey Reed, how's it going? You and Taz still having fun in the sun?"

Reed snorted. "No, we've had enough of that. Dad's doing a lot better. We just got home, actually. We'll be in tomorrow. I wanted to check in with you and see if there was anything that needed my attention before then."

"Not really. Everything's fine here." Peter was his usual calm, even-tempered self. Reed was glad some things stayed the same and he could count on them. "Oh well, come to think of it, there was something."

Damn, he knew it. Too good to be true. "What's that?" Reed cautiously asked.

"Two people came in today, and they were looking for Taz."

Reed's blood ran cold. Holy Mother of God. Who did Taz even know in New York outside of him and Peter? Could it be… did that nasty Vorlod guy come back? If so, why?

But wait, Peter said two people? Had he brought reinforcements to take Taz away from him? Over his dead body.

"Did these guys say why they were looking for him?" Reed asked.

"Not guys. One guy. One woman. And no, they didn't really say. The guy seemed to have a stick up his ass, and the woman was on the bossy side. Is something wrong?"

"I hope not. We'll see you tomorrow, Peter. Thanks for everything. You're the best."

He disconnected and turned to Taz, forcing himself to smile. He wasn't going to worry his kitten about this, not until he had to. Let him get a good night's sleep first. Before Taz could even ask, they heard another knock. Reed realized with relief that dinner was there. That would provide the perfect distraction. The rest he'd worry about tomorrow.

FOURTEEN

THE NEXT morning was the usual three-ring circus of making sure Taz didn't drink too much coffee, dressing more quickly than Taz could get Reed undressed, then flagging down a taxi to go to his poor, neglected shop.

"I'm glad to be back." Taz's attention was repeatedly drawn to the taxi's window while he sipped at the coffee that Reed had fixed for them. It was his second cup and his last one. At least for now. He could probably inveigle one later, if he was careful not to bounce too much.

"Me too." Reed smiled as Taz glanced out the window again. "See something interesting out there?"

"Not as interesting as what's in here." Taz looked at Reed and winked. Despite his bottomless interest in this world filled with humans, nothing was as fascinating as the human across from him. "It's just.... Everyone is so busy here, always on the go. There is energy here I didn't notice in Florida."

"Things move at a much slower pace in the South. This...." Reed waved his hand. "This can take some getting used to, especially if you aren't from the area. In the beginning, it was overwhelming for me. But I adjusted."

Taz sighed. "It kind of reminds me of home. Except for being more above the ground."

"Oh babe, I'm sorry." Reed patted Taz's knee. "I really am. I wish there was something I could do to help, but...."

"There isn't anything. I know that." Taz covered Reed's hand with his own. There was nothing anyone could do. Didn't make it hurt less. "After seeing your family, the deep love your parents have for you and your brother and sister, I can't help missing my family. Even if my brother is a pain."

"I can understand that. I have one of those pains myself, you know."

Taz faced Reed, the people outside the taxi no longer holding his attention. "Oh no, I didn't mean it like that. Mine isn't like Jacob. He isn't homophobic. Where I come from, we don't have this silly prejudice against same-sex couples. It's a nonissue there, and no one thinks anything of it. No, my brother... how can I explain him? Calymbraeze's in the military. He's very rigid and straitlaced. He'll probably be there for life, he's that devoted to what he does."

"Ahhh, I see. From what I understand, people who dedicate their lives to serving tend to be...." Reed shrugged. "Not sure what the word is I want."

"Committed," Taz answered immediately. "But he can't help it, I guess. It's his life. I used to wish he'd loosen up some, you know?"

"You care for him, don't you?"

"Of course! He's a good guy. There's just no... fun in his life. No joy. No one to push him into easing up that control of his. At least, I don't think there is. There wasn't when I... left home. Things might have changed since then."

"I'm sorry, Taz."

"Don't be sorry, Reed. I wouldn't change a thing. You do know that, yes? You are my everything." Taz leaned forward eagerly as the taxi stopped in front of A Touch of Class. "I can't wait to see Peter."

Reed paid the fare, then followed Taz out of the taxi. "I imagine he can't wait to see us either."

Taz laughed softly. He knew what Reed was insinuating, but he also knew Peter was a nice guy. Taz would bet Peter would cover for Reed for as long and as many times as Reed needed him to. But yes, he also bet Peter was more than ready for a break.

Reed held the door while Taz walked into the shop, calling out, "Peter? Peter! Hey, where are you?"

Peter popped out from behind a rack of clothes. "Hey there! You're back."

REED NOTICED Peter had dark circles under his very tired-looking gray eyes, and he seemed to have lost a little weight off his almost six-foot frame.

Reed sighed. "Hey, man. I can't tell you how glad I am to see you."

Peter approached them with open arms. "How's your dad?"

Reed hugged Peter then stepped back. "He's good. It's all good now. How are you?"

"I'm good."

Reed frowned. "You sure? You look tired."

Taz hugged Peter next. "Reed worries. But he is right, you do look tired."

Peter ran a hand through his hair and laughed self-consciously. "Man, I've worked nonstop since you left. Of course I'm tired. Have to tell you guys, you're making me feel uncomfortable."

"Is that all?"

Taz glared at Reed. "Reed, don't be so—"

Peter held up his hand. "Hold on, Taz. He's just worried, that's all. Reed, I'm fine, really. I'm tired, yes. Really tired. You could say I'm exhausted, and I wouldn't disagree. I had no idea how hard running a business was. How do you do this every day and have any kind of life?"

"You just experienced what my life had turned into before I met Taz. It was all about the work. I didn't even know how unhappy or how lost I was until I found him. I just don't want to see you fall into the same rut as me."

A grin crossed Peter's face. "Well, since I don't own a business, I don't think it's going to be a problem. But I am glad you're back. I'm going on vacation. A nice long vacation."

Reed slapped Peter on the back. "Absolutely. You more than deserve it. So, did anything happen while we were gone?"

"Are you kidding me? This place runs as smooth as silk, man. The only odd thing, like I told you, were the two people looking for Taz."

Taz looked at Reed in surprise. "What? Someone was looking for me, Reed, and you didn't tell me?"

"Aw, damn." *Busted.* "Yes, I knew. Peter told me last night. I didn't tell you then because I didn't want to worry you, that's all. I wasn't going to keep it from you. I figured today was soon enough for you to get stressed out."

Taz's hands landed on his hips and he glared at Reed. "We will talk about this later, my Reed." He looked at Peter. "Can you describe them to me?"

"Well, it was a man and a woman. The lady was older than the man. She was very elegant, very well-spoken. Everything about her reeked of power, if that makes any sense. I mean, she was nice, but she made me feel like I should bow to her or something. It was weird. Anyway, she—" Peter stopped and stared at Taz. "Huh."

"What?"

"Well, come to think of it, her hair reminds me of yours, Taz. Which is odd because I've never seen anyone with your hair color before. Anyway, the guy was standoffish and kind of uptight. He was pretty tall too. At least six inches taller than me. And he was a ginger. What's really a shame was this guy was sexy as hell, but I just bet he squeaks when he walks, you know? He's that uptight and aloof, like he's always holding himself in. Personally, I think he looks like he needs to get laid. In the worse way." Peter smirked. "And tell you what, I'd be more than happy to help him out, trust me. Hell, I'll even supply the lube."

A grin lit up Taz's face, and then he laughed outright. "This man, he looked like he had a stick stuck up his ass, yes, Peter? That's how Reed describes—"

"Damn, Taz." Reed interrupted, looking around. "Good thing the shop's empty."

Taz clapped his hands together, eyes shining. "Oh, it won't be, not for long. Not if I'm right."

Reed glanced at Taz. "Huh?"

Peter rolled his eyes. "Want to try that again, and in English, Taz?"

Before Taz could reply, the door popped open and almost as if on cue, a couple entered the shop—a tall redheaded man and an older woman. They seemed to match Peter's description of them to a tee.

Taz jumped up and down excitedly, bouncing on his toes. "Oh, stars. Oh, stars! I can't... I can't believe.... Oh *stars*! Mom!"

"Mom?" Reed gasped. He exchanged startled looks with Peter. Although Reed was certainly the more startled of the two, since he alone knew just how far Taz's family must have traveled to be here. And how had they managed to find him? Questions crowded his head thick and fast as he watched Taz leap across the room, lift his mother, and spin her in a circle before setting her back onto her feet.

The next thing Reed knew, Taz was dragging his mother across the floor, while his brother—at least he assumed that was Taz's brother—followed them a little more warily.

"There is someone you must meet, someone wonderful."

It took a second for Reed to realize that Taz was talking about him, and that he was about to meet his future mother-in-law and brother-in-law, and dear God, was this really happening right here and now? It would have been nice to have some sort of warning. To be prepared for this. Holy cow.

He was so flustered, he missed part of what Taz said until he heard his name.

"Reed is my husband-to-be," Taz finished with a flourish. He took his place beside Reed and placed his arm around him. Three pairs of eyes all turned to stare at the couple.

What a way to announce an engagement, Reed thought.

Peter was the first to break the somewhat awkward silence. "That's wonderful! Congrats you two! When's the happy day?"

"Um... um... um.... We don't know," Reed stammered. He'd expected Peter's approval. What he was worried about was Taz's family. And there was still the whole story of how the hell they knew where to find him on a planet the size of Earth.

That was the point at which Taz's family all began speaking at once, a confused jumble of sounds that made no sense to Reed. He wasn't sure if it was because his head was spinning or because they were using their native language, whatever that might be.

Taz's mother raised her hands and clapped them twice, sharply. Both her sons fell silent. Reed gave her an admiring glance. He would have to remember that tactic in future.

"We will dine together," she announced in a commanding voice. "And we will get to know Fabrintazo's intended."

It took a moment for Reed to realize that Fabrintazo meant Taz. *What a mouthful. Just like his kitten. Oops.* He filed that thought away for later. *Not in front of his mother.*

They were tourists. Of course they wanted to eat out. But was that such a good idea? Reed looked at Taz uneasily. He wasn't sure that getting takeout and bringing it back to the apartment was any better of an idea.

Then the brother stepped into the picture somehow, and the next thing Reed knew, Peter was waving them out the door of the shop with the admonition to have a nice lunch, and they were all getting in a cab to find just the right restaurant. Guilt at leaving Peter holding the bag again suffused Reed.

What else could this day bring? And was he going to be able to survive it? After doing a little brainstorming with himself, Reed finally suggested a little Italian restaurant he knew that was off the beaten path. It wasn't the fanciest place in town, but it had a homey atmosphere, great food, and excellent service. It also didn't require a reservation. Or a black tie. The visual that thought produced... all he needed was for Taz to mention ties and what they did with them and Reed knew he'd simply die of embarrassment.

Maybe with a little luck, he'd be able to get a table in the back corner somewhere.

Reed cringed at his thoughts, but he couldn't help himself. Did Taz's mother and brother understand Earthlings didn't know about them—them being aliens? It had taken Taz time to adjust to monitoring his speech, and Reed still worried at times that Taz would mess up and say something that might give him away. What if they acted like what they really were—visiting aliens from another planet? People would either think they were completely crazy, or they'd believe them. Reed didn't know which idea scared him more.

Power seemed to cloak Taz's mom, power that set his nerves to twitching. He wasn't sure what the lady did, or who she was on their planet, but he'd bet his bottom dollar she was someone important. His brother's appearance, on the other hand, shouted that he was some type of soldier or a member of the military. There was power there too, especially in the way—oh, what was his name? Calymbraeze—held himself. And the mother's name was Marjayla. He really needed to remember that.

Reed gritted his teeth as they arrived at the restaurant, absently rubbing his stomach. As much as he loved the food here, there was no way he was going to be able to eat. It was bad enough meeting Taz's mother when he hadn't had a chance to ready himself, but throw in his mom was an alien and this had all the makings of a first-class nightmare. Reed entered the restaurant first and had a quick word with the hostess. His luck was holding. There was a table available in the back, away from everyone.

Taz grabbed Reed's arm and held him back as the hostess led them through the tables of the other diners, to their own spot near the kitchen. After everyone had passed, Taz leaned close and whispered, "They know to be careful."

"Are you sure?" Reed whispered back.

"They've been coming to Earth for a long time." Taz winked at Reed. "Both Mom and Cal are much more… conservative than me. They both hold important positions on our home. I'll explain more to you later, but for now please stop worrying. It'll be fine." He took Reed's hand in his own and squeezed it reassuringly.

"Still, I'd much rather have done this at our apartment. And maybe had several weeks to prepare. That would have been good." Reed blew out a breath. "Jesus, Taz, were you this nervous about meeting my parents?"

"A little. But I knew it was important to you. And I also knew you wouldn't let them hurt me. It all turned out okay, didn't it? Your parents were great and so was Renee. I love them all. My family will love you too."

"How the hell did they find you, Taz? Not that I'm not thrilled for you, but...." Reed shrugged, knowing full well he was green around the gills. "What do they want?"

Taz reached for Reed's hand. "My place is with you, my Reed. If that's what's worrying you, then be at peace. I'm not leaving you. Now or ever."

Reed swallowed. Trust his kitten to get right to the heart of things. "Can they make you?"

"Have you ever tried to make Fabrintazo do something he didn't want to do?"

Reed jerked at the sound of the new voice. Oh, great. Things just went from bad to worse. He looked up at Taz's very tall brother. Damn, he had to be around six and a half foot easy.

Calymbraeze nodded at Taz, a slight frown on his face. "I can tell you that's impossible. My little brother gives new meaning to the word stubborn."

Taz smiled. "That is true. By the way, I go by Taz, Calymbraeze. And I think it would be better to call you Cal instead of using your full name, if you know what I mean."

"Agreed." Cal turned to face Reed. "Reed, we are aware of the... political climate here. We are not stupid." Cal jerked his head at the table where Marjayla sat. "Are the two of you going to join us, now that you've had your chance to talk privately?"

Reed felt his face heat. Was that a reprimand? Damn sure sounded like one. "Look, Taz's safety is my main concern, you understand? Plus I know, firsthand, the problems he had adjusting when he first arrived here. How am I to know the two of you won't make the same mistakes he did?"

Cal hiked an eyebrow at Reed. "We… travel more than Taz. We are more aware of things concerning such travel. Not to mention that we know all about protocol. Probably more than most people of your planet."

Reed glanced nervously around at his last words. Luckily, no one was listening. "All right, then, I guess that covers that." Reed held out the chair for Taz, then sat down himself. He would cut his own tongue out before telling Taz he wasn't overly fond of his brother. He hoped it was just a bad first impression, but that remained to be seen. Jacob was an asshole. Cal, Taz's brother, acted like he had something stuck up his ass. And not in a good way.

Reed quickly pointed out what was good from the menu, unsure if they'd ever tasted Italian food before. *First time for everything, right?* The waiter came and all the orders were placed, including drinks. *Please, let there be a lot of drinks….*

Marjayla took a sip of her water, then stared at her youngest son. "So, Fabrintazo, you are planning to be mated, I understand."

Reed tried not to cringe at the word. Mated sounded like something animals did. Guess they just had a different way of saying things where they came from. What was the name of Taz's home planet? Oh yeah, Trygos. Of course he'd never tell Taz's mother that. Something about this woman was just… intimidating. How did Taz get to be the friendly soul he was living with her? Must be his father. Reed wondered where that man was, but he sure wasn't about to ask. The brother seemed more like their mother, maybe even more so. Rigid, even. Lovely. On second thought, maybe he should limit the alcohol intake. At least until he got Taz alone again.

"Yes, Reed and I are going to be married here, in New York, instead of Floorda, where Reed's Herb and Jeanette and Renee live. It's not legal there."

"Florida," Reed automatically corrected.

"Illegal?"

Reed watched the mother and brother exchange glances. Great, what a wonderful first impression. He knew what they must be thinking. Ridiculous planet, low on the evolutionary scale, why did Taz ever come here, and what can he possibly see in one of its inhabitants? The thought did nothing for his queasy stomach.

"Yes, there are some people who do not like men who love other men. Or women who love women." Taz frowned. "But some places are better than others. And here in New York, the government has given its permission to allow this."

"Sounds positively primitive," Cal declared. "I wonder if their military is as backward as their society?"

Why, do you want to invade? Reed reached for his glass and drank rather than voice the thought.

Taz's mother continued, her focus on Taz, skirting the issue entirely, for which Reed was grateful. "I tried to comm you, but you did not reply." Her voice was calm, but behind her words Reed sensed something more—concern for his well-being? Only natural, even when your child was as old as Taz, to worry when he didn't answer your call. The word comm opened up all sorts of images, mostly of the sci-fi variety. What did she mean, anyway? Did their people possess a device that allowed communication between other planets?

Reed watched Taz squirm under his mother's questioning and thought he looked downright sheepish, actually.

"The truth is… I mean…." he waffled.

"You left it at home, didn't you?" Cal supplied.

Taz nodded. "If I'd had it, I would have let you know I was stranded," Taz admitted. "But see. Everything has worked out so well! I met Reed and he is my forever mate, and now here you are! How did you ever find me?"

"You have your brother to thank for that." Marjayla nodded toward Cal. "I was concerned when I could not raise you, so we went to your school. We learned from your roommate—"

Taz had a roommate? Huh, that was news to Reed. He shook the thought off, focusing on her words instead.

"… and then your brother traced your steps to Vorlod, so he found him and questioned him closely, until he admitted you had chosen to remain on Earth."

"Chosen? I *chose* to be dumped?" Taz spluttered indignantly.

"Shhh, shhh, kitten." Reed tried to soothe his riled alien, stroking his hand gently. He glanced around, but no one seemed to be paying them any attention, thank God. "It's all right, we know that's not true."

"He brought me to this planet on false pretenses, just so he could make eyes at Truba," Taz huffed. "Then he left me with no way home and no clothes other than what I wore and not even a good-bye."

Reed slid his chair closer to Taz. The rest of the diners be damned, his kitten was upset and he needed him. Granted, he realized it was Taz's wounded vanity speaking, that he was long over what had happened. Still, he was there for him, come what may. He put a protective arm across Taz's shoulders, and Taz leaned against him. *Ah, much better.*

"He shall pay for that."

At first Reed thought Cal was talking about them, but when he glanced at him, he saw no censure in his look. Then he realized he was referring to Vorlod, the insufferable alien who had abandoned Taz on a strange planet with no way home.

Good. His brother seemed to be on Taz's side. One point for the military guy with the stick up his ass.

"That is not our way," Marjayla said simply. "We came as soon as we learned your whereabouts. I had assumed you were studying, what with being so close to your final examinations. You haven't forgotten your studies, have you?" She arched a brow at Taz.

"No, of course not." Taz sat up straighter, just as the appetizers arrived. There was a calculated silence as the server laid everything before them, asked if they needed anything else, and then withdrew.

"So, when will this mating take place?" she continued in a matter-of-fact voice that Reed couldn't help but admire. He liked the way she never flinched at the idea her son was marrying another man. What a wonderful place their planet must be in that regard if they had such universal acceptance.

It took a moment to realize that everyone was looking to him for answers, and at this time, he had none. Hell, they hadn't really had time to discuss it. Everything had happened so quickly. Not that he regretted the impulse that had led to his proposal. Certainly not. But just getting engaged was a big step, all on its own, without throwing in the rest of it. And there were his parents to consider. And the business, and Peter.

"I-I don't know," he finally admitted, feeling stupid for not knowing.

"We must wait until Herb is well enough to travel," Taz put in, for which Reed was grateful.

"Herb? Who or what is a Herb?" Cal asked.

"He's my father. And he's been... ill." He didn't want to try to explain a heart attack to two aliens. It wasn't a concept he felt all that sure of discussing with other earthlings.

Oh dear God, when had that word crept into his mindset?

"He isn't able to fly yet. Which is why we were in Florida. In fact, we just got home last night," Reed finished.

"Home?" Marjayla turned her focus back to Taz.

"Yes, home, Mother," he replied, nodding his head so enthusiastically his calico hair flew up and down. "Home is here now. Where Reed is, that is where I wish to be. And no place else."

"I see."

Reed couldn't read the tone of her voice, couldn't tell if he sensed disapproval or disappointment. He had no clue what in the hell she was thinking, and that bothered him. He didn't want his kitten to be torn in his loyalties, to feel he had to make a choice between his family and Reed. On the other hand, there was no way he wanted to be separated from Taz again. The first horrible time, when Vorlod had kidnapped him and tried to drag him back to Trygos, had been bad enough.

"So, tell me more about yourself, Reed."

Reed felt as though a moment had passed. Had the tension at the table just lessened, or was he imagining things? He could always hope.

"Not much to tell. I grew up in the South, with my parents and my brother and sister. Um, southern United States, that is." He wasn't sure how good their grasp of Earth geography was, but he sure as hell wasn't about to ask.

"My sister's name is Renee, she's a couple of years older than me, and she runs her own business in Florida. My brother Jacob lives there too. He's older than I am. What else?" He got a momentary reprieve as the server returned with the main course, and the dishes were swapped out. He hoped that the matter was forgotten, but Marjayla nodded at him, as if to say go on. So he did. He noted, with approval, that Taz was eating. So things must be okay, right?

"I got my bachelor's in Primary Education, but I didn't really get a chance to use it down there. I ended up coming to New York and opening A Touch of Class. I employ a few people, and the shop is actually doing pretty well. That's about it, I guess. That's me pretty much in a nutshell." He glanced at Taz as if to confirm that he'd given all necessary information, and received a nod of approval.

"I'm not sure about the nutshell," Taz admitted, "but that is my Reed, the most wonderful person I've ever met."

Reed felt his heart warm at such extravagant praise.

"Where did you two meet?" Taz's mother asked.

"At the Empire State Building. That's where Vorlod dumped me, and that is where I fell on Reed."

"You *fell* on him?"

Was that a muffled laugh he heard? Reed didn't trust his ears. And yet… he could have sworn he'd heard it. Cal, on the other hand, did not seem amused. Not angry, simply disapproving. Taz was right. That man needed to lighten up, and a good boning would probably do him some good too.

Jeez, when did he start measuring everything by the amount of sex one got? That answer was easy—ever since he'd fallen in love and lust with Taz. He sincerely hoped neither Taz's mother nor brother was telepathic, as the images that flooded his mind just then were purely pornographic. He hastily thrust them aside.

"Yes, I fell on him, and then I apologized, and I told him I was hungry, and he offered to feed me. And he introduced me to a very special beverage on this planet. It's called coffee. Have you heard of it?"

"Oh yes, I've heard of it." She gave Reed a look. "I hope you've had the presence of mind to limit him to decaffeinated?"

"Weeellll." Reed managed to make the one syllable sound like several as he stretched it out. "I didn't realize that I needed to. But now we limit his daily intake, just to be safe," he hastily amended.

Calymbraeze snorted. "That's probably the smartest thing you could have chosen to do. My brother has a great tendency to bounce as it is without adding the effects of your caffeine. We have no such thing on Trygos, and no need for it."

"Oh, but it is wonderful," Taz objected. "So warm and delicious, and the cream that we put into it comes in so many wonderful flavors. I love the one that tastes like a cinnamon bun. That's my favorite. I will make you some when we go to our home, and you will see how delicious it is."

What? Did Taz just invite them over for coffee? Reed began to panic slightly. What condition was the apartment in? Had they dumped everything in the living room on their arrival, or had they put it all away? He couldn't think straight.

"We had not thought to stay so long." That was his mother. Reed gave an internal sigh of relief, until he saw the look of dismay that crossed Taz's face. *What's the matter with me?* Of course Taz would be sad. He'd been missing his family and here they were, so Reed shouldn't be glad to be getting rid of them so quickly. He felt like a real heel for not thinking more of Taz's feelings.

"Don't leave," he surprised himself by saying. "I mean, you just got here and all. And Taz has missed you. Surely you can stay a bit longer?"

"I have an idea!" Taz clapped his hands together.

Uh-oh, he's getting that look in his eyes. Reed tried not to groan as he asked, "What idea is that, babe?"

"I want to show them our special place," Taz said.

Oh good. He was going to take three—count 'em folks, three aliens, not just one—to the Empire State Building. He wondered when life had become so complex. But then he realized that happened when Taz entered it. And he wouldn't have it any other way.

"I'm not sure we can get in," he waffled, but the die was cast, and once dinner was consumed and paid for, they found themselves in a taxi heading to arguably one of the most infamous and well-known destinations in New York City.

He felt childish for doing it, but he crossed his fingers on the way over that they'd missed the last car of the evening, but no such luck. They were just in time, and before he knew it, they were all assembled on the observation platform where he'd first met Taz.

Taz showed his mother and brother the spot where he'd fallen on Reed, and Reed tried not to blush too much. Then he took them to gaze out the window to get the effect of the lights, which tonight were red and orange in hue.

"We have no such structures at home," Marjayla admitted.

"No we don't, do we?" Taz jumped in with enthusiasm. "That is what I have been trying to explain to people on Trygos, but no one listens. The best buildings rise from the ground, gracefully, beautifully, like this one. To build underground is not a proper utilization of the space that we've been given to live in."

"And that is why you will be an architect, my son." Marjayla patted Taz's cheek, and Reed detected more than a little pride in her voice, which endeared her to him all the more.

When she turned toward him abruptly, he was taken by surprise, caught up in thoughts of Taz as he was.

"We will be leaving you, but not for long. Only until the wedding."

"Only until... the wedding?" Reed stammered stupidly. *Huh?*

"Of course we must wait until your father can fly. It would be silly otherwise. Your family must be present at your marriage as much as Taz's. Once I return home, I will begin arrangements. Oh, and before I forget." She reached into a jacket pocket Reed hadn't noticed before and pulled out a metallic object about the rough size of a cell phone.

"I have brought your comm, so now we shall be able to talk whenever we want."

When Reed was a lot younger, he'd taken a dare from some friends to jump out of his bedroom window. It had seemed a good idea at the time. And they'd laid an old mattress on the ground beneath the window to cushion his fall. Granted, he'd had a first-floor bedroom, and it wasn't a great distance. But he still remembered the way the breath had left his body when he jumped, the way he'd felt like for a split second he had ceased to exist. Until he hit the mattress and it all came rushing back to him.

That's how he felt now. Like he was falling and couldn't stop, and his head and stomach were spinning, and nothing he could do or say would stop what was coming.

And then it came.

"In three of your Earth months, everything shall be ready," she announced.

What would be ready?

"Taz, Calymbraeze shall stand for you, of course. And that man we met today in your shop, Reed. What was his name?"

"Peter," Reed replied from numb lips.

"Yes, he shall stand for you...."

Good God, did that mean what he thought it did?

"And your parents, of course. And your brother and sister."

Reed turned panic-stricken eyes to Taz, who seemed elated. He seemed happier than mere happy—he fairly glowed.

"Oh stars, how wonderful!" He threw his arm around Reed and hugged him tightly. "We're getting married on Trygos! And with all your family and mine!"

Oh Lord, how the hell was Reed even going to begin to explain this to his family and Peter? He managed a weak smile before he buried his face against Taz's neck.

Never mind. They'd find a way. He could do this, surely. If Taz could forsake his home world to become a part of Reed's, surely Reed could marry Taz and be his human forever.

He held Taz closer to him and counted to ten slowly. Yes indeed, tomorrow was another day. And as long as he had Taz, he was sure he could survive it.

JULIE LYNN HAYES was reading at the age of two and writing by the age of nine and always wanted to be a writer when she grew up. Two marriages, five children, and more than forty years later, that is still her dream. She blames her younger daughters for introducing her to yaoi and the world of M/M love, a world which has captured her imagination and her heart and fueled her writing in ways she'd never dreamed of before. She especially loves stories of two men finding true love and happiness in one another's arms and is a great believer in happily ever after. She lives in St. Louis with her daughter Sarah and her cat Ramesses, loves books and movies, and hopes to be a world traveler some day. She enjoys crafts, such as crocheting and cross stitch, knitting and needlepoint, and loves to cook. While working a temporary day job, she continues to write her books and stories and reviews, which she posts in various places on the Internet. Her family thinks she is a bit off, but she doesn't mind. Marching to the beat of one's own drummer is a good thing, after all. Her published works can be found at Dreamspinner Press, Amber Quill Press, Torquere Press, and eXtasy Books.

By JULIE LYNN HAYES

Yes, He's My Ex

MOONLIT SKIES (WITH M.A. CHURCH)
Be My Alien
Be My Human

Published by DREAMSPINNER PRESS
http://www.dreamspinnerpress.com

M.A. CHURCH lives in the southern United States and spent many years in the elementary education sector. She is married to her high school sweetheart and they have two children. Her hobbies are gardening, walking, attending flea markets, watching professional football, racing, and spending time with her family on the lake.

But her most beloved hobby was reading. Even at an early age she can remember hunting for books at the library. Later nonhuman and science fiction genres captured her attention and drew her into the world the authors had created. But always at the back of her mind was that one day, when the kids were older and she had more time, she would write a book.

By sheer chance she stumbled across a gay male romance story on the web and was hooked. A new world opened up and she fell in love. Thus the journey started. When not writing or researching, she enjoys reading the latest erotic and mainstream romance novels.

Visit M.A. at her blog http://machurch00.blogspot.com or e-mail her at nomoretears00@hotmail.com.

By M.A. CHURCH

Shadows in the Night
Wrapped in Leather

MOONLIT SKIES (WITH JULIE LYNN HAYES)
Be My Alien
Be My Human

THE GODS SERIES
Priceless
Perfect
Pure

Published by DREAMSPINNER PRESS
http://www.dreamspinnerpress.com

Read how it all got started in

BE MY ALIEN

MOONLIT SKIES

M.A. CHURCH
JULIE LYNN HAYES

Julie Lynn Hayes

YES, He's My EX

http://www.dreamspinnerpress.com

The Gods series

http://www.dreamspinnerpress.com

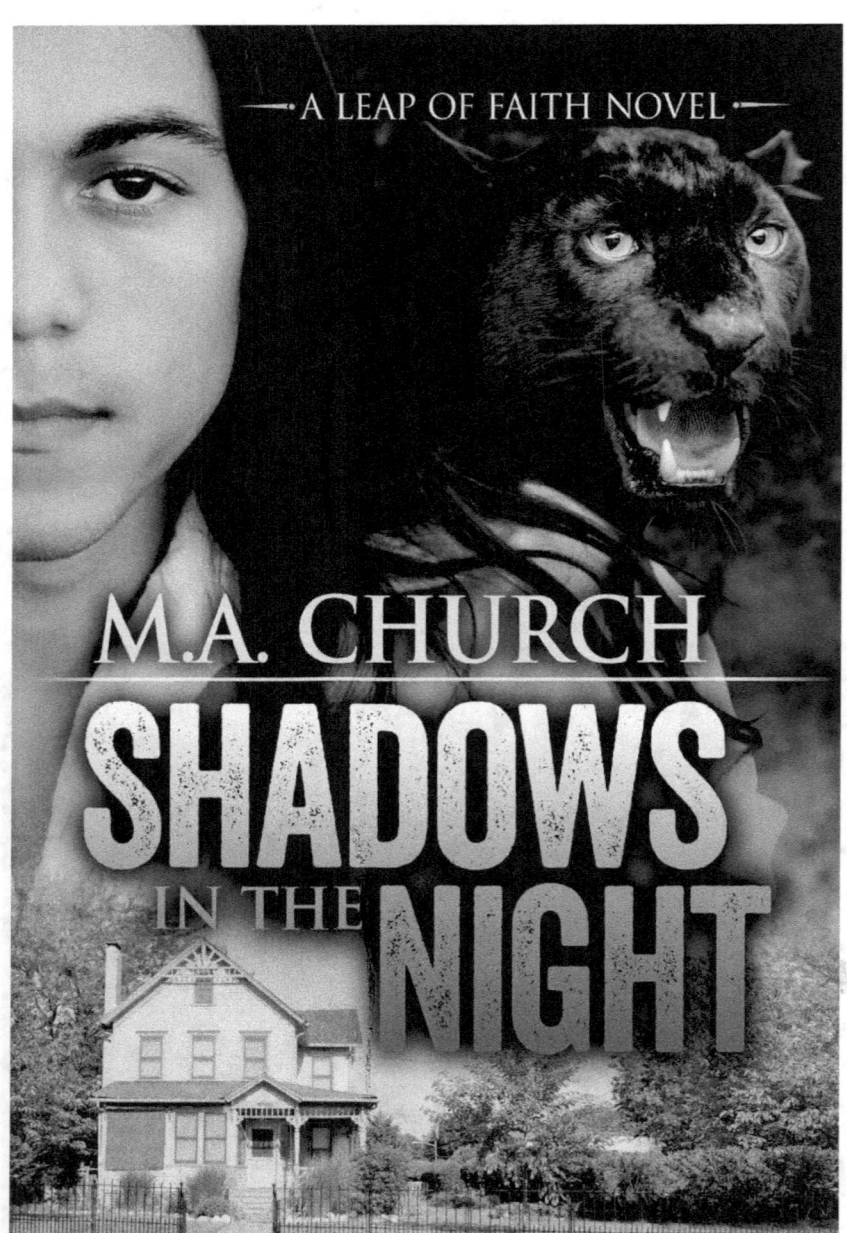

A LEAP OF FAITH NOVEL

M.A. CHURCH

SHADOWS
IN THE NIGHT

http://www.dreamspinnerpress.com

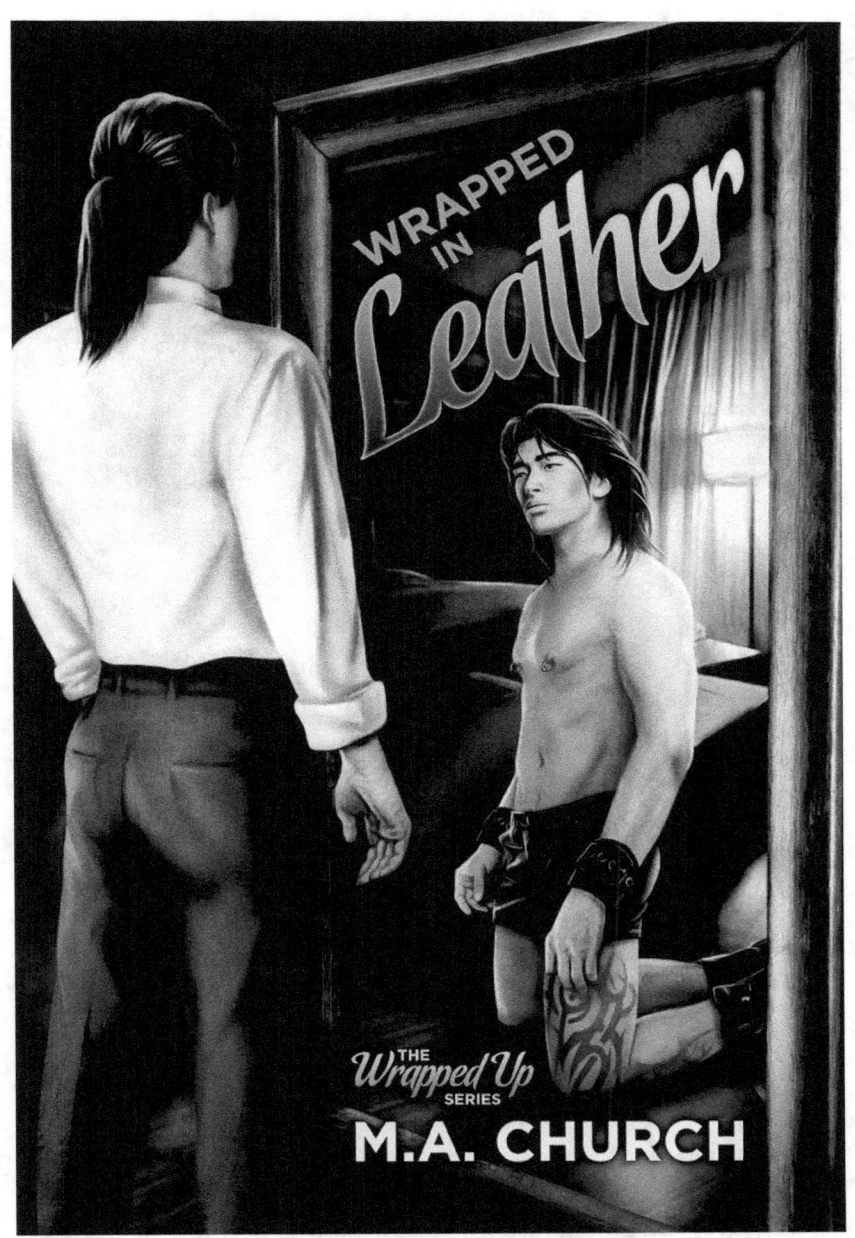

WRAPPED IN *Leather*

THE *Wrapped Up* SERIES

M.A. CHURCH

http://www.dreamspinnerpress.com